SOS

TITANIC

EVE BUNTING

SOS TITANIC

HARCOURT BRACE & COMPANY

SAN DIEGO   NEW YORK   LONDON

Requests for permission to make copies of any part of the
work should be mailed to: Permissions Department,
Harcourt Brace & Company, 6277 Sea Harbor Drive,
Orlando, Florida 32887-6777.

Library of Congress Cataloging-in-Publication Data
Bunting, Eve, 1928–
SOS Titanic/Eve Bunting.
p.   cm.
Summary: Fifteen-year-old Barry O'Neill, traveling
from Ireland to America on the maiden voyage of the
Titanic, finds his life endangered when the ship
hits an iceberg and begins to sink.
ISBN 0-15-200271-5   ISBN 0-15-201305-9 (pbk.)
1. Titanic (Steamship)—Juvenile fiction. [1. Titanic
(Steamship)—Fiction. 2. Ocean liners—Fiction.
3. Shipwrecks—Fiction.] I. Title.
PZ7.B91527Saad   1996
[Fic]—dc20   95-10712

The text was set in Galliard.
Designed by Camilla Filancia
First edition
A B C D E   A B C D E (pbk.)

PRINTED IN HONG KONG

To the memory

of those who died on the RMS *Titanic*

AUTHOR'S NOTE

This is a fictional story, an adventure set on board the ill-fated RMS *Titanic*. I have tried to be as accurate as possible with the positions of decks, cabins, stairways, et cetera; but details of the layout of the *Titanic* are complex, and photographs are few. She sailed on her maiden voyage April 10, 1912. She sank in the North Atlantic five days later, April 15, 1912, at 2:20 A.M. Her life was short.

Many of the names in this novel are names of real people, such as Phillips, the wireless operator. It was he who switched from the traditional distress signal CQD to the newly designated call, SOS. This was the first time in history the distress call SOS was ever sent.

Some of the names and events I used are purely fictional. I tried only to tell a story, one of the hundreds that might have happened on that first, and only, tragic voyage of the RMS *Titanic*.

—E. B.

SOS

TITANIC

With a boom loud as gunfire, and then another, great chunks of ice broke free of the glacier and splashed into the dark sea. Gulls shrieked and rose. A seal curved itself and dove as the newly birthed bergs settled in the seething ocean and drifted silently south toward the shipping lanes.

Barry O'Neill stood on the Queenstown quay, along with Mr. Scollins and Grandmother and Grandpop. In the last minutes before the leaving, the quay swarmed with excitement. People from the town were there, and some who'd come in from the country to share the

< 1 >

thrill of the big ship's maiden voyage. It had been built in the Belfast shipyard and launched in Southampton, and was on its way to New York. There'd never been a ship like it in the history of the world. There would never be a sailing like this one again.

It wasn't very hard to tell the watchers from the goers. The watchers were having a holiday. But for the goers and their relatives this wasn't just another day with midday dinner brought in a basket and the chance of a few hours without rain. This was the end of the old and the start of the new. This was adventure, good or bad. They stood in small clusters, silent and subdued.

Barry and Mr. Scollins were two of the goers.

Barry tightened his throat to hold back his tears. Hard enough for his grandparents, without him having a blatherfit and making things worse.

He glanced sideways at the Flynns. They stood together in a pushing, noisy bunch. There were his archenemies, Jonnie and Frank Flynn, surrounded by all

< 2 >

the other brothers and sisters. There was Mrs. Flynn, her hair coming out of a streaky bun, flowered apron drifting below her black coat. There was Mr. Flynn, in the same old trousers and bald wool jacket he'd worn all week long, for cutting turf on Saturday, for going to mass on Sunday.

As if sensing Barry's look, Jonnie spoke to Frank and the two of them glared, their dark Flynn scowls flying at him like black crows. One of the sisters turned, too, the one with red hair thick as a horse's tail, and she gave Barry a scornful up-and-down stare. Was she the sister who was going to America with Jonnie and Frank? She might be. The three of them had on new, stiff clothes, the fold marks still showing in them, and their boots were shiny and unscratched.

"We'll be on the same ship with you, Master O'Neill," Jonnie Flynn had said the day they'd come upon each other in front of the blacksmith shop. "Bad cess to your grandfather for making me leave Ireland. It was because of him that the others decided to come, too. They'd never let me go alone. We Flynns stick together."

< 3 >

"My grandfather didn't make anybody leave," Barry said fiercely.

"It was him, and you along with him. And here's something you should think about. There'll be the three of us—Franky, me, Pegeen—and only one of you. You haven't had the pleasure of meeting our sister Pegeen, but you will like her. Why wouldn't you, seeing as how she's just like me and Frank?"

Jonnie had been speaking in the high-falutin' voice he always used when he talked to Barry, the little talking that they did. *As if I can help the way I speak,* Barry thought. *As if I haven't tried to lose the boarding school voice that comes from talking that way every day of my life since I was five years old and sent to London to the Chesterton School for Boys.* He had only had the holidays with Grandmother and Grandpop to strengthen the Irish that was part of his heritage.

"I'm just as Irish as you are, so you can drop that accent," he'd yelled one day at Jonnie Flynn. "My ancestors have been here for . . . since . . . for centuries and centuries, longer than yours."

< 4 >

"My kind doesn't *have* ancestors," Jonnie Flynn had sneered, scuffing off down the footpath in his loose boots, which had strings for laces.

They would all be on the same ship for the whole voyage, even though Barry and Mr. Scollins would be in first class and the Flynns would surely be in steerage. There'd be a confrontation. Well, he wasn't going to worry about them. Maybe Mr. Scollins would prove to be an ally on board the ship—though looking at him, Barry didn't think he'd be much of a help in a fight.

"Barry"—his grandmother bent forward to take a piece of lint off his dark coat—"you'll be very careful, won't you?"

"Yes, Grandmother."

"And, Mr. Scollins—I don't need to tell you this, I know, but grandmothers worry, so I trust you'll forgive me. Please take good care of our grandson." She tried to make her voice light. Barry knew that way she had of saying something serious and making it seem unimportant. "We want him to be looking fit and healthy when he meets his mother and father in New York, so they'll know we've

< 5 >

taken good care of him all these years. So maybe they'll let him come back and visit."

"Of course they'll know that, Grandmother. You and Grandpop have always been . . ." He had to stop because the tears were squeezing up past the tightness of his throat. In a minute they'd pour right out of him.

"Never you fear, Mrs. O'Neill," Mr. Scollins said in his precise manner. "I will keep an eye on him at all times."

"Well, now." Grandpop gave Barry a wink. "A fifteen-year-old boy does need a little freedom. Don't be too strict with him. We want him to enjoy the voyage."

"Here comes the tender," Mr. Scollins said, and they all turned to see the *Pride of Erin* chugging toward them across the last few yards of open water. She was a good-sized boat that could carry upward of a hundred passengers. Tom Henderson stood on the bow, ready to throw the thick lines, and men on the dock waited to secure them safely to the hawsers.

The crowd grew silent. "Ladies and gentlemen, the baggage is safely aboard,"

< 6 >

Tom Henderson shouted. "I'll be taking the passengers to the ship momentarily."

Such a silence then, such a tense, waiting silence.

"Well, this is it." Mr. Scollins's voice had lost its stuffiness, and excitement trembled through. Hard to remember sometimes that Mr. Scollins was only nineteen, Barry thought. Not much older than Barry was himself.

He had been one of the young men who answered the ad Grandmother and Grandpop had placed in *The Irish Times*:

Responsible companion-guardian for 15-year-old boy traveling by steamship from Queenstown, Ireland, to New York. First-class ticket and five guineas provided to suitable applicant.

They had interviewed nine others besides Mr. Scollins, then they'd pronounced him the most suitable applicant: not too old to be very stern, yet old enough to be trusted—for hadn't he been working with a firm of jewelers in Dublin for five years? And wasn't it fortunate and by the grace of God that his firm was

< 7 >

expanding to America and he'd been offered a job there?

The *Pride of Erin* was moored now,
fastened fore and aft. The harbor surge
moved her gently against the row of old
oak fenders that lined the quay.

There was a sudden, terrible wail from
the clustered Flynns, and Barry saw the
mother, her arms wound tightly around
Jonnie and Frank and the girl who must
be Pegeen. "I'll not be letting you go!"
the mother shouted. "God save us, how
can I be letting you go, my own wee
children?"

"Looks as though she has plenty of
children, and some to spare," Mr. Scollins
said in his stuck-up voice.

Mr. Flynn was stroking his wife's hair,
murmuring to her. But some of the little
Flynn children were wailing now, too,
clinging to the hem of their mother's coat
or holding on to the black-stockinged legs
of the red-haired sister. "Pegeen, Pegeen,
don't go!" they screamed.

"Ah, poor things. I feel for them."
Grandmother took a handkerchief from
the pocket of her coat and wiped her eyes.

< 8 >

"Children going, mothers left behind. It's terrible hard. Could we give them a lift home, Seamus?" she asked Grandpop.

Barry touched Grandmother's hand. She didn't know, and Grandpop didn't know either, that they'd had anything to do with the Flynn children leaving.

Grandpop raised his eyebrows. "Take the holy all of them? There's not that much room in any carriage yet built. And don't be forgetting what those Flynn boys did to my carriage, and it brand-new. The big scratch along it is there yet, no matter how much Dickie polishes it."

It was Grandpop's report about the scrape that had finally turned the court against Jonnie Flynn. "Twenty-three complaints, young man. And this one just the final straw. Take your choice. The jailhouse or out of the country."

"I meant only to take the poor mother and father. They didn't do anything. There's room now that Barry and Mr. Scollins . . ." Grandmother's voice trailed away.

Tom Henderson had come to shuffle about in front of them, his navy blue cap

< 9 >

in his hand. "Madam, sir. It's time for the young gentlemen to come now. I'd like them to lead the way, being as how they're the only first-class passengers we have going out of Queenstown."

"The only ones?" Grandpop asked.

"There's four going second class, and the rest are in steerage," Tom Henderson said.

Grandmother's chin quivered. "It is time, then."

Mr. Scollins lifted the small Gladstone bag he'd insisted on keeping with him.

As if on cue, a loud blast from the big ship's funnel echoed across the ocean and rolled over them, so they clapped their hands to their ears: it set the horses that waited with the carriages and carts on the edge of the quay to whinnying and snorting.

Every head turned to look in the direction of the sound. There the ship lay, motionless, the small shapes of the passengers who had boarded at Southampton or Cherbourg dark along her rails, her four funnels big as factory smokestacks. Oh, the gleaming newness of her! Oh, the sheen and the shine! The biggest ocean-

< 10 >

going vessel in the world. Too huge to even get into Queenstown Harbor. Waiting out there, she seemed to fill the horizon and the world.

Some of the passengers began walking slowly toward the *Pride of Erin*, which would take them out to her. Walking forward but looking back as they went. Barry shook Grandpop's hand, knowing they were both crying, glad when Grandpop pulled him close so that they didn't have to see each other.

"You'll be coming home again someday," Grandpop whispered.

"Yes," Barry said.

"Your hands are like ice." Grandpop fumbled in his pockets and pulled out his old gray knitted gloves, the wool matted and thick. "Take these. They'll keep you warm."

Barry nodded.

Then it was Grandmother's turn. She hugged him against her. He smelled the old tea-rose smell that was always about her, felt the softness of the fur tippet that was draped around her neck. "Don't forget us, Barry. We love you dearly."

"I'll never forget you. Never."

< *11* >

He was sniffling and sobbing, though he'd promised himself he wouldn't, clutching the old worn gloves as he stumbled behind Mr. Scollins to where the tender waited.

"Let me hold that bag for you till you get on," Tommy Henderson told Mr. Scollins.

"No, don't touch it at all. I'll take care of it myself." Mr. Scollins held the small Gladstone bag against his chest.

"All right, then, you two gentlemen sit here. You'll be first off as well as first on."

They sat where he pointed.

The tender was filling quickly, few wanting to go but none wanting to be left behind. The Flynns were among the last aboard.

Barry realized he'd been watching for them. The girl, Pegeen, had been crying, too. Her eyelids were softened with tears. "Poor things," Grandmother had said. "Poor . . ."

"What are you gawking at, you galoot?" Frank Flynn shouted. "Keep your eyes in front of you, where they belong."

"Where I keep my eyes—," Barry began.

< *12* >

Jonnie Flynn interrupted. "I have a question for ya. Can ya swim?"

"What?" Barry asked.

"Nothing, just a question." Jonnie Flynn smiled.

The *Erin*'s engines roared to a start. Her bow started the wide circle that would turn her around and take her to the harbor mouth, where the ship waited.

Could he swim? What kind of a deadly question was that?

Barry kept looking back at Grandmother and Grandpop. Grandpop waved his hat, Grandmother her handkerchief. They were getting smaller and smaller now. Behind them, on the edge of the quay, he saw horses and carriages and carts, and he saw Dickie, the manservant who drove for Grandpop. And he saw Blossom and Midnight, their two mares. Blossom had a white splash like a flower in the middle of her forehead.

Barry swallowed hard. He didn't want to leave. He didn't. Everything, every person he loved, was here in Ireland. What did he care about going to New York, to live in a place called Brooklyn with those

< 13 >

two strangers who were his parents? Nothing.

In the end, though, all the arguments had failed. He was going. Grandmother and Grandpop were just two specks now among the other specks on the dock.

The sun, which had been hidden by clouds, came blinking through, filling the harbor with sparkles, turning the town into a fairy-tale place. The fields behind were velvety green. Those brown dots were cows—maybe O'Neill cows. On the faraway dock the crowd was singing. The words and the melody came drifting toward them the way snow flurries drift in the wind, coming easy, then stronger:

Will ye no' come back again?
Better loved ye'll never be.
Will ye no' come back again?

Barry looked up at the side of the ocean-going liner that towered over them, dark and steep as the black cliffs of Moher. A gangplank hung over the side. On the bow, in white letters almost as big as he was tall, was the name RMS *Titanic*.

"We're here," Tom Henderson said.

< 14 >

As Tom Henderson had promised, Barry and Mr. Scollins were first up the gangplank. The railings along the top deck of the ship were already crowded with passengers. In the still ocean air Barry could hear some of the conversations above him.

"They say they're all traveling steerage . . . immigrants, you know."

An American voice then, a woman's, saying, "Wouldn't you wonder why they want to leave here? It looks so peaceful and beautiful. I wish we could have extended our trip, Walter. I would love to have taken in Ireland."

And a man answering, "It would be all

< 15 >

right for a vacation, sweetheart, but you'd hate it if you had to live there."

Is that so? Barry thought. *Speak for yourself, you yahoo.*

Stewards in white jackets with brass buttons waited at the top of the gangway. One of them stepped forward, notebook in hand. He was the smallest man Barry had ever seen, with hair as black and shiny as his little pointed black shoes. *Boot polish,* Barry thought quickly. *On the shoes and on the hair, too.*

"You'll be Master O'Neill and Mr. Scollins?" he asked. And when Scollins nodded, he said, "My name is Watley. I'll be your cabin steward. If you will kindly follow me . . . May I take your bag, Mr. Scollins?"

"Thank you, no," Scollins said. "I will carry it myself."

Barry glanced back, looking for the Flynns, and he found them by the blaze of Pegeen's hair. They'd been last onto the tender, and they were last off. For a moment he watched Pegeen climb the gleaming gangway, which said White Star, Ltd. in big letters along its railing. Once

< *16* >

she stopped and looked across the Queenstown Harbor, and Barry saw her shoulders slump. Behind her, Frank Flynn put a hand to her waist. *Plenty of us happy to be going, but plenty of us sad*, Barry thought.

He and Mr. Scollins followed Watley along the lower deck, then inside and up a wide carpeted stairway where everything smelled new and luxurious, along white corridors as hushed and quiet as the corridors of the big Dublin hotels where he had often stayed with Grandmother and Grandpop. Those had always held the smell of damp and mildew—maybe even of mice. To Barry those Dublin hotels meant holidays. Would he ever know them again?

From behind some of the cabin doors they passed came the murmur of people talking. Music drifted softly. Had the voices on the Queenstown quay died away, or was "Will ye no' come back again . . ." still wailing across the harbor? Barry bit his lips. He would be back. He'd keep telling himself that.

"Here we are, gentlemen." The

< 17 >

steward opened the cabin door and stood aside for them to enter.

The cabin was large, with a mahogany dresser, a table with a tasseled lamp in the center, and two wingback chairs. Bigger by far than Barry's dorm room at school, bigger than his bedroom at home. There were two graceful four-poster beds edged with red brocade curtains, looped back now, but full enough to be closed for privacy.

"I have already unpacked for you gentlemen," Watley said. "Is there anything else you require?" His smile was like the smile of a ventriloquist's doll and never left his face, even when he talked.

"I don't think we require anything else at the moment." Mr. Scollins's superior voice plainly said that he was used to having his every need met, his unpacking done for him—and instantly.

"If you *do* require my services . . ." Watley touched a discreet bell by the door. "We will be sailing in about a half hour. You might like to go up on the boat deck for your last glimpse of the shoreline. 'Twill be a while before we see land

< 18 >

again—but sooner than we expect, if Captain Smith gets us up to full speed. We're looking to set a record for a transatlantic trip."

"Where are the third-class passengers?" Barry asked.

"Third class, sir?" Watley's smile stayed put even while his eyebrows arched.

"There's a family there from my town," Barry said.

"The steerage passengers have accommodation on the lower decks," Watley said. "Males and females are separated, though, so the girls and women will be below in the stern, the men in the bow. I doubt if you'll see much of them till we land, sir. There's no coming and going, if you know what I mean. Mixing is not permitted."

Barry was surprised by the quick sense of relief he felt. "What stops the mixing?"

"We have notices on the gates that divide first, second, and third class," Watley said. "The wording makes it quite clear where passengers may and may not go." He paused. "Some of the first-class passengers on transatlantic vessels like to go

< 19 >

down to steerage for a lark. I believe they call it slumming, and of course that is perfectly permissible." His smile never wavered. "Third-class passengers, though, may never come up here. That would not be tolerated."

"Quite," Mr. Scollins said.

It might not be tolerated, Barry thought, but unless all those gates were locked and without a gap in them, they wouldn't bother Jonnie and Frank Flynn. Not for a minute. There hadn't been a barbed-wire fence or a padlock in the whole of Mullinmore that they couldn't go over or under or through. Gentlemanly notices weren't going to stop them, or Pegeen either. Hadn't Jonnie told him she was just like them?

They'd be up. They'd be searching first class for him. "Can ya swim?" Jonnie had asked.

Mr. Scollins set his Gladstone bag on the table but kept a grip on the handle.

"One thing," he said to Watley. "I need to have this kept in a secure place during the voyage."

"Certainly, sir. I can take it straight-

< 20 >

away to the purser's office, where it can be locked in his safe."

"Thank you, but I will take it myself."

"Perhaps I would suggest that you wait, then, until after we sail," Watley said. "It's going to be rather chaotic for a while."

As soon as he left, Scollins said, "I have strict instructions from my employers never to let this bag out of my hands until it's safely locked away. And I intend to follow their orders." He lowered his voice as if he feared eavesdroppers. "This bag contains jewels. I must say, I was deeply honored that my firm entrusted them to me." He paused. "My firm, Billings and Fetters, Jewellers, O'Connell Street? You know them?"

"No," Barry said.

"Dublin's most prestigious jewelry company," Scollins said accusingly. "You must know them. Everybody does. They had planned on hiring an agent to bring these to the newly opened branch in New York. Then when they decided I was going to work for them in New York, it solved that problem. In the time that I

< 21 >

have been in their employ, they have recognized that I am eminently trustworthy. They are killing two birds, so to speak, with one stone." His glance flicked to Barry. "They're also paying me a modest sum, which will be helpful to me as I start my new life."

Another five guineas, Barry thought. *Scollins knows how to make a pound or two for himself on the side.*

"Shall we find our way to the promenade deck?" Scollins asked. "One should, I suppose, wave good-bye to Ireland. And good riddance to it, I say."

"Well, I don't say," Barry told him. "If I could stay in Ireland . . ." He stopped. What was the use? He'd never be able to talk to Mr. Scollins or tell him how he felt. He'd never want to. The truth was that those in steerage were the ones who'd understand. Not the Flynns, but others like them. Reasonable ones. They'd be the ones he could cry with. He pulled on Grandpop's gloves, ignoring Scollins's look of disgust and the tone of his voice when he asked, "Do you think you'll need those?"

"I think I'll need them," Barry said.

< 22 >

They went up a different wide stair-case, all oak and wrought iron, passing the first-class dining salon on the way. Barry saw the tables with their white linen cloths, the silver and crystal already set for the evening meal. The walls were hung with tapestries; the chandeliers glittered. Was it possible this was a ship? There was no movement. No feeling of ocean around them or under them.

As if to reassure him, one of the fun-nels blew a mighty blast.

"We'd better hurry," Mr. Scollins said. "Sounds as if we're ready to go."

They walked faster, finding space for themselves against the railings on the boat deck. Next to them was a woman in a dark red coat and a black hat with cherries around the brim.

Mr. Scollins cradled the Gladstone bag against his chest as he peered out at the water. The woman gave Barry a friendly smile. "I don't imagine this sailing will be as exciting as when we left Southampton," she said.

"I wouldn't know," Barry said. "We just boarded here at Queenstown."

< 23 >

"Oh, then you missed the fun," the woman told him. "We almost collided with another ship. Just cleared it by inches, actually." She made a face at the man beside her, who was wearing a black overcoat and a bowler hat. "My husband thought it a bad omen," she whispered loudly, "but I thought it was jolly exciting."

The man turned and smiled at her.

"He's been reading that book, you know. *Futility?*" Her whisper was still loud and teasing. "So of course he's expecting the worst."

"What book would that be, madam?" Scollins asked haughtily.

"Oh, some tiresome old book written ten or twenty years ago."

"Fourteen years ago," her husband corrected.

"It's about a ship called the *Titan*." She rolled her eyes. "It—she—was supposed to be the most wonderful ship ever built, and she was on her maiden voyage and she was hit by an iceberg and sank." The woman lowered her voice dramatically. "Everybody *perished*. Isn't that right,

< 24 >

Howard? Howard thinks it's a psychic's prediction. We're all going to end up *perished.*"

Howard glanced down at her. Barry could tell he was not quite so amused anymore. She squeezed Howard's hand and said, "I'm only joking, of course."

"Well, it could never happen to this ship," Scollins said. "This is the *Titanic,* not the *Titan.* This ship is unsinkable. She has sixteen bulkheads, each with a watertight door. In an emergency . . ."

Howard turned a withering glance on Mr. Scollins. "Never say never, young man. And don't quote statistics at me. I have a bad feeling about this ship. She's unlucky. Some of her crew felt it, too, and deserted before the sailing. If it weren't that my wife was so keen . . ."

There was another, louder blast from the *Titanic*'s funnel, and Howard's wife clapped her hands to her ears, laughing and giving little happy hops. Her black hat with the cherries on it slipped to the side, and she took one hand from her ear to set it right, laughing even more. "We're moving. We're moving!" she shouted,

< 25 >

standing on tiptoe to kiss Howard's cheek. "Oh, Howard, thank you for bringing me. It's going to be wonderful. Thank you."

Howard smiled and put his arm around her waist.

The *Titanic* was on her way.

The Flynns were probably on the deck below, watching, too, Barry thought. Feeling maybe the way he was feeling. In a way, he and Jonnie had both been forced to leave Ireland. Did that give them something in common?

Howard's wife touched his arm. "Are you Irish? I would have thought English."

"Irish," Barry said.

"Are you going on a visit, or are you leaving?"

"Leaving." The word came, gravelly, past the tightness in his throat. What a terrible sound it had.

"It must be hard," she said softly. He wished she wouldn't sound so gentle . . .

Would his mother have a voice like this? He'd seen her only three times since Father's business interests had taken them to live in China. He couldn't remember

< 26 >

how his mother sounded. He could hardly remember how she looked.

"New York, Barry," she'd written. "A wonderful move for your father, and a civilized place to bring you up. We're going to be together. We'll be a family at last."

Howard was speaking over Barry's head, talking to Scollins.

"Did you know there's a mummy in the hold of this ship? A mummy with a curse on its head?"

"Oh, Howard." His wife was laughing again. "You are such a glum old thing. Curse, indeed. Pay no attention to him," she said, waving her fingers at Scollins and Barry as they left the railing. "Ta-ta. See you again."

Scollins sniffed. "What a silly, superstitious man."

Barry didn't answer. He was watching the coast of Ireland fading in the mist behind them, watching a seagull that glided alongside the *Titanic,* then caught the wind under its wings and wheeled back toward shore. Lucky, lucky seagull, to go where it pleased. Stay where it wanted.

In front of him a man leaned close to

< 27 >

the railing. Hanging on brackets beside him was a large white life belt with the words RMS *Titanic* printed around its curve. The man moved, and one of his legs covered the last two letters, so it read RMS *Titan*.

If I were superstitious, Barry thought . . .

< 28 >

Barry and Mr. Scollins were late getting to the grand dining salon for dinner. First they visited the purser's office to secure Mr. Scollins's bag. Scollins insisted on a confirmation letter saying Purser McElroy had received it into his custody. Several people were waiting behind them to check their own valuables, and Barry sensed their impatience. Scollins was in no hurry. None of your property is as important as what I am carrying, his manner said.

"I'm afraid I'm going to be somewhat of an annoyance during the voyage," he told the purser. "My company wants me

< 29 >

to check on my bag every day. It's not that they lack faith in the White Star Line and its employees, I assure you. It is a simple matter of security."

"You must do what you think best," Purser McElroy said rather stiffly. "But I assure you, there is no cause for concern."

"Nevertheless." Scollins tucked the key of the bag carefully in his waistcoat pocket and huffed away.

"He must be carrying the Star of India," a woman said sarcastically as they passed.

"Your servant, madam," Scollins said, and bowed.

In the dining salon the chief steward led them to their table. They were seated with a young woman, Mrs. Adair, and her small daughter, Jocelyn. There was another gentleman, Colonel Sapp. Barry thought he was the little girl's father, and he felt sorry for her. Sapp was one of the worst names he'd ever heard in his life, about equal to the name of a boy in school called Charlie Twitt. Little Jocelyn would be called Sappy. Other girls would say, "Here comes the Sapp." But at least she

< 30 >

was a girl, not a boy. Girls were probably kinder, he decided. But hadn't Jonnie Flynn said Pegeen was just like him? A fighting Flynn like the rest of them?

The round table could have seated six, but there were just the five of them. Dining stewards hovered, unfolding their white serviettes and placing them in their laps. Barry looked about. He'd never been in a dining room this elegant. If he concentrated, he could feel the soft sway of the ship. *Rocked in the lap of luxury,* he thought, and the idea made him smile.

None of the passengers wore evening dress, and he was glad to have had the guidance of Watley, who'd laid their starched white shirts out on their beds and said smoothly, "I'm sure you know that no one dresses for dinner the first night out, gentlemen. So I've taken the liberty of putting out fresh linens, on the chance that you might like to freshen up." Smart, tactful Watley, with his unsurpassable White Star service.

The dining salon was like a club. People knew each other. Greetings were exchanged between the tables.

< 31 >

"Mabel, how nice to see you again. When was the last time we met?"

"The Cannes Regatta, was it?"

"Oh, no, my dear. Wasn't it spring, at the baths at Baden-Baden? Weren't you with the Cavendishes?"

Even Barry knew someone. The lady who'd worn the hat with the cherries waved cheerfully to him from two tables over. She wasn't wearing the hat now, but her gray dress had a bunch of cherries at the throat.

"I see we haven't perished yet," she called. "Howard's rather disappointed."

Howard smiled a tight-lipped smile.

"Lovely atmosphere," Colonel Sapp murmured. "Lovely. Isn't that Henry Sleeper Harper of the New York publishing family? I'm sure it is. Those are the Astors at that center table. Such a handsome couple."

"I'm afraid my friend Mr. O'Neill and I are more conversant with Dublin society," Mr. Scollins said frigidly.

"And why are you going to New York?" Colonel Sapp asked Barry, spooning up a little of his turtle soup, on which cream floated soft as snow.

< 32 >

"I am going to join my parents," Barry said, and hoped he wouldn't be asked more.

"I'm visiting a cousin in Philadelphia," the colonel said, and wiped his mustache on his starched serviette. "Robert lives in a rather exclusive neighborhood, I'm told. Bryn Mawr."

The woman, Mrs. Adair, sat quietly. Once, when she looked directly at him, Barry noticed that her right eye twitched at the corner. Twitched and twitched. He bent his head over his soup dish, trying not to meet her eyes again, but the twitch was like a magnet and as hard to ignore.

"The Adairs are going to be with her mother in Boston," the colonel volunteered. "And what of your husband, Mrs. Adair? You haven't mentioned him."

Flick, flick, flick. "Mr. Adair was unable to come with us," the woman said.

Barry wanted to rub his own eye in sympathy.

Little Jocelyn sat still as a statue.

Mr. Scollins told about his transfer to the new branch of his firm. Each time he related where he was going and what he was doing, his position grew more

< 33 >

important. By now he was a top executive with Billings and Fetters Jewellers. By the time he got to New York he'd probably be a full partner. Barry noticed that Scollins never told why Barry was with him. One would have thought he was keeping an eye on this lad as a personal favor to a friend, to hear him tell it. There was no mention of the five guineas.

The stewards changed the plates so silently that it was almost a surprise to look down and find one dish removed and another in its place.

Barry listened to the well-mannered tinkling of the glasses, to the soft laughter and conversation, to the faint distant throb of the giant engines. Hard to imagine that beyond these damask-covered walls, below the double-bottomed steel hull, lay an ocean filled with creatures with teeth and tentacles who lived their lives in those dark depths. What was that hymn they used to sing in Sunday service? "O hear us when we pray to thee, for those in peril on the sea?" Of course, whoever wrote that wrote it before the *Titanic* was built. Before the imaginary *Titan,* too.

< 34 >

The dining stewards pushed the great serving carts laden with silver dishes and domed covers through the salon. From under the domes, platters of golden duck appeared; the ducks were doused in brandy and set alight, to the ohs and ahs of the diners. The smell reminded Barry of home. Of Grandpop sipping brandy as he sat in his big chair by the fire, the wind blowing down the chimney, filling the room with the blue smokiness of the smoldering turf.

"Those are the Ryersons," Colonel Sapp murmured, leaning across the table. "I hear they brought sixteen trunks. She is always terribly well dressed, and I expect she wants to keep it up."

"You seem to be very much in the know, Colonel," Mrs. Adair said gently. Her brown eyes flicked—flick, flick, flick.

"I like to take stock of my traveling companions," Colonel Sapp told her. "One must keep up one's standards."

"Quite," Mr. Scollins agreed.

Barry smiled across the table at little Jocelyn. He thought she was probably about seven. Her hair was long and fawn colored, like her mother's. It was tied back

< 35 >

with a great navy blue bow that perched like a giant butterfly at the nape of her neck. He thought he'd never seen a sadder little face. Her lips drooped. She barely spoke except to answer her mother, yes or no. She ate almost nothing, not even the wonderful sweet of fresh strawberries and real Devonshire cream. The stewards fussed over her, asking if she'd fancy something different. There'd be no trouble to get it for her from the kitchens. A slice of chocolate cake, perhaps? She shook her head so feebly that the butterfly bow didn't even quiver.

Barry put a blob of Devonshire cream on his nose and made a face at her, but she didn't smile.

Instead, she screamed suddenly, "I want my daddy," and burst into a storm of tears. Everyone stared as she jumped up from her chair.

Her mother rose, too, making little soothing noises, her hands reaching toward her daughter. "Come, sweetheart. Mother—"

"Go away." Jocelyn shoved her little fists against her mother's chest. "I don't want you. I want my daddy."

< 36 >

Barry and Scollins and the colonel stood, too—the colonel taking a step away, perhaps to indicate that he wasn't associated with the screaming child in any way.

The Ryersons and the Astors were glancing in their direction—glancing because they were too polite to stare. The two other children in the salon, well dressed and well mannered, traveling with their parents, were very interested. One even stood on her own chair so she could see better, but her father made her get down.

Mrs. Adair's face had turned the color of the pale lace at the neck of her dress. "Please forgive us." She took the little girl firmly by the shoulders.

"Shall we bring your coffee to your cabin, madam?" the steward asked, White Star to the end. "And perhaps a hot lemonade for the little girl?"

"Nothing, thank you." Mrs. Adair pushed Jocelyn ahead of her toward the doors.

The little girl's voice, shrill as a shrike's, knifed back across the room. "You took me. You stole me from my daddy. You're mean and horrible."

< 37 >

In the silence that came after her outburst Barry could hear the small creaking of the giant ship, the subdued tinkle of china in the kitchens beyond, the faraway heartbeat of the engines.

"The perfect ruination of a good meal," Colonel Sapp grumbled. "I shall ask to have my table changed."

"There should be a special dining room for children," Scollins agreed, seating himself again, spreading his serviette quickly over his dark trousers.

"I understand there is one for the maids and the valets," the colonel said. "Why can't the children eat with them?" He lowered his voice. "I heard Mr. Henry Sleeper Harper brought his own dragoman. That's the way to travel."

"You Sapp," Barry said under his breath. He couldn't put Jocelyn's big, sad eyes, her mother's pale face out of his mind. What was wrong? How could a mother have stolen her child?

When he looked across at the two empty seats he saw that Jocelyn had left her serviette neatly folded on her chair. But, no, it wasn't a serviette, it was something else.

< 38 >

"Excuse me," he murmured, and went around the table and picked up a man's folded linen handkerchief with the initial *P* embroidered in one corner.

"Excuse me," he said again, without bothering to answer Scollins's quick "Where are you going?" or to worry about the colonel's "People will think we have the most undesirable table in the whole dining room."

Too bad, Sappy, Barry thought, hurrying toward the doors.

Outside on the veranda the string orchestra was playing a Strauss waltz, one of Grandmother's favorites. Above his head the glass dome that covered the grand staircase quivered slightly, with a sound like bells. The ornate cherub clock in its oval recess showed ten minutes to nine. Had they gone immediately to their cabin? And which cabin was it? He could keep the handkerchief till tomorrow, but he thought Jocelyn would miss it and that would make her sadder than ever.

At the bottom of the staircase he saw them. "Jocelyn," he called, "Jocelyn, you forgot something."

They stopped and Barry held up the

< 39 >

handkerchief and ran down the remaining steps.

"Why, it's one of Peter's." Mrs. Adair's mouth tightened; her eye twitched.

Jocelyn snatched the handkerchief from Barry's hand. "My daddy's," she said, and held the handkerchief to her face.

"Oh, darling girl," Mrs. Adair whispered, and put both arms around her daughter. "I'm so sorry it had to be this way. I'm so sorry."

There was so much love and pain in her face that Barry had to look away.

"Thank you," she said to Barry. He watched them walk along the corridor, and he thought he knew how Jocelyn felt. He hadn't lost his father, but he had lost Grandmother and Grandpop. If he had one of Grandmother's handkerchiefs, he would hold it against his face, too.

Behind him he heard Scollins's voice. "What do you think you're doing, young man, dashing off like that? You heard me promise your grandmother that I'd keep an eye on you."

< 40 >

"I'm not going to jump ship," Barry said. "Believe me, you're not going to lose me." *Unless Jonnie Flynn finds me,* he thought.

Scollins's face was the strange gray-white of blotting paper and there was a sheen on it as if he'd just shined it up with a soft duster.

"Suppose . . . suppose . . ." Scollins seemed to be having trouble keeping his thoughts together. "Does it seem rather warm in here?" he asked.

"No," Barry said. "It seems just right."

"I think perhaps that food was a little rich for me," Scollins said. "I must remember to be more moderate." He took out his watch, glanced at it, and said, "At any rate, we should turn in. It has been rather a long day." He eased a finger inside his starched collar. "Do you fancy a breath of sea air first?"

"Fine." They went back up the stairs and Barry pushed open the doors that led onto the wide boat deck. He and Mr. Scollins stood in the shadow of one of the high-slung lifeboats, feeling the cold, cold

< 41 >

North Atlantic wind cutting through their jackets and shirts, through their skin to the shivering bones. The sea was calm and black, except close to the ship, where the lights shone on the surface, turning it to bottle green. The sky blazed with stars. Barry pointed upward. "Gemini— Heavenly Twins," he said. "I've never seen them so bright."

Scollins rubbed his hands along his arms. "Perhaps we should move before we freeze where we stand." He strode along the deck, wavering a little, as if he felt the roll of the *Titanic;* though up here in the open air Barry felt no movement at all. There was only that throb beneath their feet.

Music was coming from somewhere, happy, dancing music, and voices, too, singing and laughing. The farther Barry and Scollins walked, the louder the music got.

"The steerage passengers must be having a party," Mr. Scollins said. "Let's turn back."

"Oh, I'd like to have a look," Barry said. Scollins might have been rented to keep an eye on him, but that didn't mean he could order Barry around, did it?

< 42 >

"Oh, very well. Just for a minute, then."

They leaned on the railing at the stern of the ship, looking down onto the deck below. It was a steerage party. A man sat on the bulkhead, playing an accordion. He wore a soft felt hat with a feather in the side, and his shirt was buttoned to the neck. A pipe smoked in his mouth and the wind carried the smell of it toward them; carried the music that squeezed out between his hands, sweet and filled with memories.

Beside him a girl stood playing a mouth organ, one foot in its black boot tapping out the rhythm. Barry saw the breeze blow a mass of red hair, and the black shawl tied around her waist. Pegeen Flynn! But where were her brothers? He looked for them in the crowd and couldn't find them.

"Down there is what's called the poop deck," Scollins said in his know-it-all manner. "Very small. But what can you expect? It only costs thirty-five pounds from Ireland to New York if you're willing to go steerage."

< 43 >

"Or *have* to go steerage," Barry said. He leaned farther out.

The music had quickened now. It was the kind you heard at celebrations back home. The small space below them swarmed with dancers. Skirts and shawls billowed. Sleeves ballooned. Boots thumped. There was laughter, and words called out in a language he couldn't understand—Swedish, maybe, or German. He knew the Irish words, though, and there were plenty of them. There was singing and he knew the song:

> *Have you ever been in love, me boys, and*
> *   have you felt the pain?*
> *I'd rather be in jail myself than be in*
> *   love again.*
> *For the girl I loved was beautiful,*
> *   I want you all to know,*
> *And I met her in the garden where the*
> *   praties grow.*

Barry wished he was down there singing along with them.

"I really don't feel well at all," Scollins said. "I think . . . " He put his hand across his mouth and began walking quickly back the way they had come. With his free hand

< 44 >

he waved urgently for Barry to follow him.

What if I don't? Barry thought. What could Scollins do, after all—complain to Grandpop? Not for a while, he couldn't.

"I think I'll stay here and watch," Barry said.

"No, no, no." Scollins clutched at one of the stanchions that held the lifeboats high above their heads. "I insist."

I won't go, Barry thought. Scollins wasn't about to carry him, or have him escorted to the cabin, or have him locked up in the purser's safe along with those precious jewels. But Scollins might insist on staying himself, indisposed or not.

Barry remembered the red brocade curtains that could be pulled across the beds for privacy. Perfect. If he got undressed and into bed and pulled those curtains closed behind him, Scollins would be satisfied. In fact, if Barry were careful to act obedient he could be wherever he wanted to be every night of the trip and Scollins wouldn't know the difference. He'd go now, then come back here and watch. Better than lying sleepless, imagining Grandmother and Grandpop back at home without him.

< 45 >

"I do think we'd better go to the cabin," he said, and faked a yawn. "It's getting cold."

He'd change into the heavy white sweater Grandmother had knit for him. "It's a fisherman's sweater," she'd said. "See the cable pattern? That's the O'Neill mark from years back. If an O'Neill fisherman drowned, they could tell who he was by this cable. See here, these rows of stitches looped over the others?"

Grandpop had winked. "So if the fish had eaten his face off, they'd still know him for an O'Neill."

"Stop it," Grandmother protested, shivering. "Do you always have to be so plainspoken?"

"It's my nature," Grandpop had said.

I'll change into my O'Neill sweater, Barry thought, *and the tweed cap, pulled down to hide my eyes, and Grandpop's gloves. And I'll come back up here and look down on them.*

"Looking down on us, as usual?" Jonnie Flynn would have said if he'd known.

But Jonnie Flynn would never know.

< 46 >

Barry was ready, waiting. It hadn't been easy to get one set of clothes off behind the brocade bed curtains, and another on. He'd wriggled like an eel going up the River Bann. Now he lay quietly, pretending sleep.

Scollins tossed and groaned. Once he got up and heaved into the washbasin. Barry decided there couldn't be much of that too-rich meal left, and surely soon he'd sleep.

Scollins had left his curtains open, either for air or for a dash to the washbasin if he needed it again. Through a gap in the fold of his own drape Barry watched

< 47 >

him. Scollins looked so small under the blanket, his face the color of its white fleece, his eyelids fluttering. The fringed brocade swayed back and forth with a gentle, steady rhythm as the ship plowed through the ocean under its canopy of stars.

An hour must have passed, but Barry had no thought of sleep himself. He was restless and nervous, filled with a muddle of feelings. The sorrow of the leaving, the strangeness of being on the big ocean liner. The fighting Flynns, Mr. Scollins, little Jocelyn and her mother—they all paraded through his mind. Would his mother look like Mrs. Adair? Would she have fawn-colored hair? Of course not. In the photos and in his scattered memories her hair was black, with the same wild curl that his own hair had. And his father? He had a bald spot in back that could be covered by a penny. Sometimes his father had done that, Barry remembered, balancing the penny on his head, staggering around.

He thought about the *Titan* and the *Titanic*. That was only a coincidence. There were coincidences in life. He and

< 48 >

Grandpop had the same birthday . . . One party for the two of them, and Mrs. Bowers baking her cream sponge cake with raspberry jam and presents all around.

Through his thoughts came the soft sound of snoring.

Scollins had kicked off the blanket. Barry crept out of bed and covered him again so he wouldn't get cold and wake up. Gently he closed both sets of bed curtains.

Now it must be late. Would the party on the poop deck still be going? He put on his cap and Grandpop's gloves and tiptoed out of the cabin.

The quiet voice almost startled him into letting the door bang.

"Are you having trouble sleeping, Master O'Neill? Shall I bring you a glass of warm milk?"

Watley stood there in his white steward's jacket with its brass buttons, every strand of his boot black hair perfectly in place.

"Oh, no, thanks. No milk," Barry said. Did White Star stewards stay on duty day and night? "I was awake, so I decided to

< 49 >

go out and watch the party that's going on in steerage. I know some of the people." Why did he feel he had to explain? Was Watley his guardian, too?

"Yes." Neither Watley's face nor his voice changed, but there was something hidden in both of them.

The great ship gave a sudden shudder, so that they staggered.

"What was that?" Barry asked.

"Probably a rogue wave." Watley smoothed his jacket. "Waves are like people; they don't always do what's expected of them."

Barry grinned. "But surely no wave would dare shake the *Titanic?*"

"Don't be too certain," Watley said. "The ocean always has a surprise or two waiting."

He sounded like one of those solemn mechanical fortune-tellers in the glass booths at summer fairs. Put in a penny and he'd tell you the future, standing there with his mouth not moving but the card popping out of the slot below: *You will have great good fortune. News will come from across the water.* Barry always knew

< 50 >

it would be from his mother and father, across the water and across the world.

Watley's eyes were like the fortune-teller's, too, seeing nothing, seeing everything. "Saying the ship is unsinkable is a proud statement," he went on. "And one the sea may not like." He squared his little, white-jacketed shoulders. "Excuse me, sir. I've been at sea too long. Never you worry about anything. Whatever may happen, Watley's here."

"Thank you, Watley," Barry said. "Good-night, then." *What a strange little man*, he thought. *What does he think is going to happen?*

Barry went quickly along the corridor, up the wide staircase, and out onto A Deck. It was colder there than it had been two hours earlier, and he dug his chin into the rolled neck of his sweater and paced faster. Beneath his feet the smooth wooden deck trembled, the way a drum still shivers minutes after you've finished playing it. The sea stretched black and calm to the horizon.

That was the edge of the world out there. He'd never seen the edge of the

< 51 >

world so clearly. In Mullinmore there were always trees and soft hills between you and it. But over there was where the world ended. It seemed you could step over it and be someplace else. The stars were so big that if he jumped he could pull one down and put it in his pocket or carry it, glowing, in his hand.

There was a small movement in the shadow of one of the bulkhead lights, and Barry saw a woman and a man. They'd been standing close together, but they moved apart when they saw him. Her coat was pale against the darkness of sea and sky; her hair, too.

"Lovely night," the man said. "Looks like we're going to have a fine crossing."

The woman turned her back and stared wordlessly across the ocean. "Good-night," the man said.

"Good-night."

The deck was damp. Did spray come up this far, Barry wondered, or was this the same kind of night dew that wet the grass at home? Now he could hear the music, fast and lively, rising from the deck below, and he walked even faster. "Molly's

< 52 >

Jig." They were still there, then, singing and dancing. His own feet felt like dancing along with them.

There was nobody leaning over the railing now looking down on the celebrations. The first-class passengers would be snug in the smoking room or in the Café Parisien, or down in their staterooms. A wind blew across the stern, whistling its own songs in the lines and stays. A shooting star with a ribbon for a tail raced across the sky. Barry stood a little back from the railing in the shelter of a metal post, looking down on the hurly-burly of color and movement below. This was better than lying sleepless in his bunk, thinking his sad thoughts, listening to Scollins snore.

There wasn't an inch of the small poop deck that didn't jump and dance. He saw Pegeen Flynn whirling around with a funny-looking fellow in an odd white jacket. No Jonnie Flynn to be seen. No Frank. They'd be exploring, looking for Barry maybe. *It's because of your grandfather and you, too. Bad cess to both of you. Can ya swim?*

A man in a navy blue coat, like a

< 53 >

sailor's, almost, looked straight up at him and pointed, nudging the arm of a man beside him. Instinctively Barry pulled back, forgetting the metal pole with its studding of rivets; he whacked his head against it with a thump that jarred his teeth and made his eyes water. *Jakers!* What had he done to himself? And why? Those two fellows had meant him no harm. They were laughing, probably, at the way those jackass snobs of first class looked down on steerage. And weren't the first-class fellows a dull lot altogether, in spite of their riches?

He pulled off one of his gloves, probing at his face, and felt the warm, wet trickle of blood. The gash was high on his left cheekbone and so sore he could hardly touch it. There'd be swelling, too. What a stupid . . . And that was when he realized he'd dropped the glove. Where was it?

The ship's lights shone white on the deck around his feet. There was no glove. Had it fallen? Had he somehow kicked it over the edge and into the ocean? Grandpop's glove. Or— He looked down again on the poop deck and saw it. It had fallen on a coiled rope and lay neatly in the

< 54 >

middle, like a cherry on top of a bun. Barry closed his eyes. His cheek was throbbing, but that wasn't the worst of it. The worst of it was the glove.

Suppose he called down, pointed at someone to throw it up? They'd never. He knew it surely. They'd make sport with it the way the boys at school did when they took your cap or book and tossed it around from one to the other. There was no way they'd throw something back to a first-class passenger. One who'd come to gawk at them.

What if he went down himself, then, and got it? Watley said first-class passengers sometimes did go into steerage. For a lark. He would never be noticed, not in that crowd. Not in that jumble of noise and movement. Carefully he checked again, sorting out the crowd below. Neither Jonnie nor Frank Flynn was there. They might come, though. He'd have to get down and back fast.

Metal steps at the side led straight to the poop deck. The trick would be not being noticed on the staircase. He pulled his cap lower on his head and waited.

In a few minutes the dancing stopped

< 55 >

and someone called out, "Time for a song. Will you give us a song, Sean McGinnis?"

A man in a long black coat said, "I will and all," and stood up on an overturned box and began to sing:

> *There is not in the wide world a valley so sweet*
> *As that vale in whose bosom the bright waters meet.*

There was such stillness below now. Such attention. Everyone there was leaving a Vale of Avoca or someplace equally loved—or someone loved.

Carefully, slowly, Barry undid a chain. First Class Only was printed on the other side of the sign that hung on it. He hooked the chain carefully back in place behind him and went silently down the steps.

Bad luck take it! Two people were leaning now against the coil of rope, and from below here he could see that this wasn't going to be as easy a job as he'd thought. The rope coil was bigger, wider. Wouldn't it have to be, for a ship the size of the *Titanic*? There'd be no just reach-

< 56 >

ing up and taking the glove. He'd have to climb—and not now. Not till the singing was over and the dancing started again. Not till those two people moved.

He stood back against the railing, the ship's wake spreading like a white triangle in the ocean behind him, boiling itself out into darkness.

A girl about his own age edged over beside him.

Barry stared straight ahead. *Don't talk to me,* he thought. *Don't notice me.*

"What happened to your face?" she asked.

"I fell against a post," Barry said, not looking at her.

She laughed. "You must have been falling-down drunk, then, for this ship's steady as a rock."

The singer was finishing:

Oh, the last rays of feeling and life must depart
'Ere the bloom of that beauty shall fade from my heart.

"That was good," the girl said, "but he shouldn't be singing such a sad ould

< 57 >

song. Aren't we all sad enough?" She faced him, sticking out her hand. "My name's Mary Kelly, what's yours?"

"Barry O'Neill." She had a cap like his own and hair dark as his, but spiky. The coat might have been her father's, for it trailed to her ankles and had lapels on it that stuck out from her shoulders like wings.

The music had started again and he caught a glimpse of Pegeen Flynn among the other dancers. She was still with the fellow in the fat white jacket, but now Barry saw that what he was wearing was a padded life jacket. It made him look as round as he was long, and took away his neck. He and Pegeen held each other at arm's length, swinging around and around, Pegeen's black skirt billowing like a balloon, her red hair streaking behind her.

One of the straps of the boy's life jacket swung loose, clipping people as they passed, and he stopped and refastened it. Pegeen hugged her arms around herself as if she were cold with the standing, and then she and the boy were dancing again.

< 58 >

Mary followed the steadiness of his glance. "Do you know Pegeen?"

Barry shook his head.

"I just met her tonight, myself," Mary said. "She's not a bit happy. I pushed her out there and told her to dance. She might as well; there's no turning back now. That's my brother, Mick, she's with. He's wearing that stupid life jacket because he's deadly afraid of the water. He can't swim. Well, none of us can, I suppose. He says that life jacket will be on him day and night till we reach New York."

"Good idea," Barry said, though he thought it must be uncomfortable. Imagine wearing that thing in bed. He let his gaze wander over the crowd, checking again for Jonnie and Frank, feeling himself relax when he saw there was still no sign of them.

"I told Pegeen there's not a bit of sense being mopey," Mary went on. "Of course, it's easier for me. I have my ma and da with me, and Mick as well."

The music had stopped and Pegeen and her partner stood, waiting. Barry glanced quickly at the coil of rope. From

< 59 >

here he couldn't even see the glove. But it was there, and so were the two men carrying on a serious conversation. Would it draw too much attention to himself if he just said "Excuse me" and climbed past them?

Mary was waving and shouting, "Pegeen, Mick, over here!"

Their heads turned, and Barry saw that they were coming toward him and Mary. He pulled the peak of his cap lower and began moving away.

"Don't be going now. I want you to meet my friends." Mary had a hold of his arm. She was calling out again to Pegeen. "Don't you feel better now, the both of you? This is Mr. Barry O'Neill. We'll have to get him at the dancing, too, for I think he needs a bit of cheering up."

"Barry O'Neill." Pegeen took a step backward.

And then some terrible force smashed into Barry, sending him reeling against the railing, almost cutting him in two where his kidneys would be, maybe, pounding the breath out of him.

Jonnie and Frank Flynn.

< 60 >

"He's yours, Jonnie," Frank said, and Jonnie had his fists up and he was hopping from foot to foot in his newly polished boots, shouting, "Come on, me boy, come on, me boyo. We found you at last."

Barry tried to get up, but his legs had turned soft as porridge. He crawled, stood, and was smashed down again by Jonnie Flynn's fists. His cap flew off.

"You got him a good one. Look at the blood, would you?" Frank shouted.

"He didn't do that," Barry wanted to say. "I got that from the post." But there was no wind in him to say anything.

"Give him a chance, Jonnie. Let him off the ropes," someone called.

And then a girl's voice, "It wasn't sporting of you, coming up on him secretly like that." Through the haze that filled his mind he recognized Mary Kelly's voice. His new friend. The only friend he had here—if she still was one.

Barry got up, shaking his head the way their hound, Oliver, shook his when he came through water, and he got his own fists up.

There was a crowd around them now.

< 61 >

Barry lashed out. Somehow and by good luck he found Jonnie Flynn's stomach, flailing away with both arms, pumping, getting himself far from the railing and the drop to the deck below—and below that, the drop to the cold, dark sea.

"This is for your ould rascal of a grandfather," Jonnie Flynn grunted. He threw a punch to the side of Barry's head—the good side that hadn't been cut before but might be now. A handful of stars jumped from the sky and danced around him inside the place where his brain used to be.

But the mention of his grandpop was strong as smelling salts. Barry flung himself at Jonnie Flynn's knees, both of them down now, rolling over and over on the deck.

Feet in boots and buttoned shoes and laced-up brogues stepped back to give them room. No need for gentlemen's rules. The boys were gouging, scratching, grunting words in Gaelic and in English.

And then they were being pulled apart. Someone had Barry by the back of his sweater, lifting him up. Across from him

< 62 >

Jonnie Flynn struggled in the hands of a seaman who was saying, "Easy now, boy, easy," the way Bowers, their grounds-keeper, spoke to Oliver, pulling on his collar. Barry couldn't see who was behind him. Someone big and with the smell of strong tobacco on his hands.

And standing a bit away, in the uniform with gold braid on the sleeves and on the peak of his cap, was Captain Smith.

"What's going on here?" he asked, his voice deep and dark as the ocean itself. "I won't have fighting on my ship."

His hands were in his jacket pockets. His short gray beard shot out from his chin, stiff and angry. He was fiercer looking even than the pictures Barry had seen of him. Captain Edward J. Smith. Previously in command of the *Olympic*, the *Titanic*'s sister ship, his photograph in all the newspapers in Ireland; here now, in person, scolding them.

"Mr. Feeney! Taffy!" Captain Smith said. "You may release the young gentlemen." The tobacco hands behind Barry loosened their grip.

< 63 >

The crowd was quiet, paying close attention.

"What's your name, young man?" This to Jonnie Flynn.

"Jonnie Flynn, Captain, sir." It was the same bad-mannered, insulting way of talking he had when he spoke to Barry or to Grandpop, or to Bowers or Dickie, even. It said, *I'm me and I don't give a rat's tail for any of you.*

"And you?" The captain's steady eyes examined Barry.

"He's Barry O'Neill, a toff down from first class. Down slumming," someone called. Barry thought he recognized Frank Flynn's voice.

"Got more than he bargained for," someone else added, and there was laughter and applause. Barry's face burned. He fingered the cut on his face and the swelling around his mouth.

"I dropped my glove," he said, or thought he said, through his swollen mouth.

"Huh," a voice mocked. "He came down here to make trouble."

"No, it's my grandpop's glove and it's up there in the rope. I lost it through the railing."

< 64 >

"I'll have no more of this," the captain said, as if he'd heard nothing—and maybe he hadn't. Maybe every word Barry had thought he'd said had been only inside of his head.

"You two young gentlemen—and all of you—will stay inside your classes for the rest of this voyage," Captain Smith said. "Those are the rules. You know them. They are posted on the gates and barriers. We do not tolerate disrespect for the rules. Mr. Feeney, Taffy, escort Mr. O'Neill back to his cabin. A stop off at the ship's doctor would be in order. He may need a stitch or two in that face."

He turned toward Jonnie Flynn. "And you. Have you any wounds to speak of?"

"Och, sure, he hardly touched me at all." Jonnie Flynn grinned widely. "You can't beat the Irish, Captain, sir." Barry noticed how he turned his head so the red bruise that was already darkening the side of his face was hidden.

Barry picked up his cap.

"Good-night, ladies and gentlemen," Captain Smith said, and he nodded to Barry and to the two seamen to follow him as he strode away. Barry heard the

< 65 >

laughter and cheers behind him. He heard the shouts of "You showed them, Jonnie, boy. You told them."

"It'll be a while before the English fellow comes back to tangle with the likes of us."

Barry looked back and saw Pegeen Flynn. She lay on her stomach across the coil of rope. In her hand was Grandpop's glove.

< 66 >

The ship's doctor took four stitches
in Barry's cheek.

In the infirmary mirror Barry examined
the ugly-looking gash. What would Scollins say? "How did you get that?" he'd
ask. "You were supposed to have been in
bed, asleep."

Taffy had waited with him and now
walked him back to his cabin.

"So you're going to hook up with
your mum and dad in New York," he said.
He glanced across at Barry. "I tell you
what, son. Why don't you go up to the
Marconi Room in the morning and send
your folks a telegram. Say, 'Having a

< 67 >

lovely time,' or something like that. Make you feel better, and them, too."

Barry nodded. "Thanks." A wireless wouldn't be like a letter. He wouldn't have to wonder what he could say to his mother and father to fill up the page. He'd send a wireless to Grandmother and Grandpop, as well as one to his parents.

Taffy clapped him on the back. "Good-night, then. I hope you won't be too sore to sleep."

Barry opened his hand, the one without the glove, and showed the two white tablets the doctor had given him for pain. He'd sleep.

Watley wasn't on guard in the corridor, and Barry was glad of that. He didn't want offers of hot milk, or questions either.

Mr. Scollins's bed curtains were still closed. Barry slipped into his own bed and lay thinking. Was Jonnie Flynn sleeping? Frankie? Were they planning something new? Or would they stop now? And Pegeen? What had she done with the glove? The pills made his thoughts blurry, made the *Titanic* seem to pitch and toss like a

< 68 >

small boat in a heavy sea. He laid Grand-pop's glove on his pillow by his cheek, breathing in the dog and horse and old-rain smell of the wool, and let sleep come.

It was Watley's discreet knock that wakened him in the morning.

"Good day, gentlemen. Tea?"

Barry opened his curtains and sat up. His brain felt numb, but not his face. It throbbed from ear to ear.

"Oh, dear," Watley said. "What happened, sir?" He set the tray he was carrying on the cabin table.

Scollins poked his head out like a turtle from its shell. "My heavens, did you fall out of bed?"

"No, I got up and bumped into . . ." Barry looked around and saw nothing in the cabin he could have bumped into. "You were asleep," he added quickly. "I went up to the infirmary and the doctor fixed it for me. It's nothing."

Scollins shuddered. "What will your parents say? I will get the blame."

"I'll tell them it was my fault."

< 69 >

Barry drank the tea Watley offered, but Scollins shook his head weakly and lay back on the pillows.

"Gentlemen, breakfast will be served in the dining salon in a half hour," Watley said.

And Scollins murmured, "I may stay where I am this morning."

Watley took Barry's empty cup. "Better to keep away from that part of the ship, Mr. O'Neill," he murmured.

"What was that?" Scollins asked.

"I was advising Mr. O'Neill to be careful not to slip." Watley's everlasting smile was in place. "If you have no further need of me . . . ?"

"No," Barry said, "and thanks. That is good advice, Mr. Watley."

He dressed quickly.

"You just have a quiet day, Mr. Scollins," he said. "Rest."

Mrs. Adair and Jocelyn were not at breakfast either.

"Having it in their cabin, I expect," Colonel Sapp said. "Lazy habit, breakfast in bed. Never could tolerate it myself." He forked kippers and scrambled eggs into

< 70 >

his mouth. "Good God, man, what happened to you?"

"A shark bit me," Barry said. If he was going to be asked the same question by everyone, he should have a better answer ready.

The colonel guffawed and sprayed kipper morsels across the table. "And that pasty-looking fellow you're with? Did the sharks swallow him in one bite? He's not much of a seagoing man, I expect. Weak stomach."

"I'm afraid so." Barry allowed the dining steward to spread a serviette across his lap and take his order.

"Wouldn't have had a fellow like him in my regiment," the colonel said. Amidst spattering kipper showers he told Barry how he himself had been attacked once, not by a shark, but by a tiger. "An unhealthy-looking beast. Mange, most likely."

Barry only half listened, examining the knife at his place. It was of heavy silver, with the White Star logo etched on the handle. What if he slipped it into his pocket? At least he'd have a weapon if the

< 71 >

Flynns found him again. But that knife was too long, and the bread-and-butter one too small. Useless with its blunted point and flat edge.

"Excuse me," he told the colonel, interrupting a story about another daring escape. "I have to go to the Marconi Room to send a wireless home."

The first-class shop was on his way. Its windows were filled with all kinds of *Titanic* souvenirs: caps and trousers and elegant scarves. Instantly Barry spotted the small penknives, their ivory handles etched with the ship's image. He went inside and asked to see one. There was a notch at the edge of the blade so you could put your thumbnail to it and pry it out. It fit tightly, but if he nudged it just right it slid out easily. The point was sharp and the edge fine-tuned. Could he use it if he had to? If someone were pushing him over the railing into the cold, dark ocean he could.

He was sweating, and he wiped his face with the back of his hand. The pig stickers came to Mullinmore every year at butchering time. You could hear the squeals all over the village as the pigs' throats were

< 72 >

cut, even down in the woods where Barry went to cover his ears. Would he be able to stick a knife in anyone? *Yes,* he told himself. *If I have to.*

"One shilling and sixpence," the smiling clerk said. "It is rather a sweet little souvenir."

On the counter was a basket half filled with silver whistles on chains. They were the kind that policemen carried and blew when they needed help—one had shrilled all through Mullinmore the day Jonnie Flynn had grabbed a woman's hat from McKee the draper's and ran with it. "I'll take this, too," Barry said. "How much?"

"Ninepence. Aren't they nice?" She picked one up and gave it a polite little toot. Barry hoped he could make more noise with it than that.

Outside the shop he put the knife in his pocket and the whistle around his neck, letting it hang cold and hard inside his shirt. If he unbuttoned the second button, he could pull it out fast.

He practiced opening the knife blade one-handed as he walked. *Quick draw,* he thought. *And I'll get quicker.*

< 73 >

The Marconi Room was jammed with bodies. If he blew his whistle here, now! Barry grinned and felt the jagged edges of the stitches cut into his skin. He'd have to remember not to smile until this healed up.

What were all these people doing here anyway? It was like the club room at the Bantry horse races. He jammed himself in at the back. Between the heads he could see the wireless operator at his desk, black earphones in place, sparks flying from under his fingers as he tapped out messages on the set in front of him. The room surged with excitement and impatience. Behind the counter, filling in wireless forms, was another man, younger than the operator. "Yes, sir. Certainly, sir. As quickly as we can," he kept saying over and over. The "in" basket where he put the completed message forms was bulging to overflowing.

"Can you do one right away, Mr. Phillips?" the young man called over his shoulder to the operator. "It's urgent." Barry got a glimpse of the wireless operator's pale face as he turned and stretched

< 74 >

to ease his shoulder muscles. "What is the message, Mr. Bride?" he asked, his voice thick with weariness.

"It's a stock-exchange quotation," Bride, the counterman, said. Barry imagined him rolling his eyes at the operator, safely knowing the passengers behind him couldn't see.

"Bring it here," Mr. Phillips said. "I'll get to it just as quickly as I can."

Conversations raced around Barry. "I'm sending a wire to Percy Harbington. He was supposed to be on this crossing but his polo pony got sick."

"Ah, bad luck."

"They say Captain Smith's out to make a record crossing."

The wireless operator was calling again to Mr. Bride. "Message just came in that needs to be taken to the bridge." He rubbed his forehead. "I don't expect you can get away just yet. Take it up as soon as you can."

Mr. Bride nodded. The operator stuck the wireless message on the spiked file beside him, which was already topsy-turvy with paper. Barry edged himself to the side

< 75 >

and tried to read the bulletin for the bridge. It was upside down and skewered sideways; he could only understand part of it. Something about the weather and icebergs. There was a longitude and latitude reading. He imagined one great liner calling to another across the endless green ocean, the words skipping on the surface of the water like stones bobbed across Donnelly's pond. Exciting. Mysterious.

They'd be passing icebergs. With any luck he'd get to see one.

While he waited he passed the time opening and closing the little knife in his pocket, getting the feel of it. He tested the sharpness of its point on his finger. He could do it.

Mr. and Mrs. Cherry Hat were sending messages. So was Mrs. Jacob Astor. She wore a fur tippet that Barry thought wasn't nearly as nice as Grandmother's. It was made of two foxes that hung down her back, their black beady eyes staring at everyone, their claws spread. Poor dead foxes.

It was almost lunchtime when he got to the counter and filled in his wireless

< 76 >

forms. The communication for the bridge was still stuck on the spike. He could see a corner of it under the mountains of speared papers. Maybe he should offer to take it up to the captain. "Captain Smith," he'd say, "remember me?" No, they'd never trust him with it anyway. He concentrated on filling in the lined wireless forms. "Having a great time. Love, Barry." The same words for all of them, but the love he sent wasn't the same.

He hurried then, knowing he'd be late again to the dining salon. The colonel would be miffed.

Their table was filled. Mr. Scollins, pale and pasty, was having a cup of clear soup and some dry crackers. Colonel Sapp noisily spooned up something thick and dark brown with cream that floated on top. Turtle soup again, maybe. The ladies had joined them, Mrs. Adair with her pale hair braided in a coil that sat high on her head like a crown.

Little Jocelyn was the only one who didn't look up when Barry came. She was wearing a jacket with a furry lamb for a pocket. Barry saw how the lamb bulged.

< 77 >

Inside would be her father's handkerchief. He knew it. He knew without being told that she carried it everywhere. And he remembered last night, the comfort of his grandfather's glove on the pillow beside him.

The dining steward unfolded Barry's serviette, placed it in his lap, and offered a menu.

"My word, what happened to you?" Mrs. Adair asked. And for the first time Jocelyn looked up.

Barry bared his teeth at her. "A shark," he said. "He jumped up and over the railing. I was way up on A Deck, too. And he had teeth THIS long." He spread his arms. "And when he opened his mouth . . . "

"My mother hit my father once on his head," Jocelyn said clearly. "He had to have eleven stitches. He had to have the whole of his hair shaved off."

They all sat in a stunned silence. Even the colonel stopped drinking his soup.

"My mother's bad," Jocelyn added.

"Baby, please!" Mrs. Adair's eyelid went flick, flick.

< 78 >

The steward, still hovering with the menu, said discreetly, "Have you decided on your order, Mr. O'Neill?"

"Ah. Oh. The fish." Barry pointed to the printed menu. "Usually at home we have fish on Friday," he added to no one in particular. "At school, too."

"Good for you," the colonel observed. "Gives you brains, what?"

"*Sole meunière*. Thank you, sir," the steward said.

"Are you feeling better, Mr. Scollins?" Barry asked, forcing his glance away from Mrs. Adair's face, which had been pink a few moments ago and was now as pale as the ivory profile on Grandmother's cameo brooch.

"I'm a little better," Scollins said stiffly. "I have already been to the purser's office and checked on my bag." He sounded accusing, as if Barry should have taken care of that for him. "This afternoon I plan to sit on deck and take the air," he went on. "I'd be obliged if you'd stay with me, Mr. O'Neill. I feel reluctant to let you out of my sight, day or night."

Barry made another shark face at

< 79 >

Jocelyn. "Want to come on deck and sit with us?" he asked her. "Maybe the shark will come back. You could have a look at him."

Jocelyn gave a little giggle.

"Or we could play cards," Barry offered. "Do you like to play 'Go to Duck Hill'?"

"I don't know it," Jocelyn said.

"It's easy. I'll—"

Her mother interrupted. "I'm afraid Jocelyn needs to take her nap this afternoon."

Or you don't want her to talk to me, Barry thought. *Who knows what secrets she might tell?* Jocelyn's hand had crept into the lamb pocket and stayed there.

Mr. Scollins brought up the subject of Jocelyn and her parents as he and Barry sat on the deck. The stewards had found them long wooden deck chairs and tucked White Star blankets snugly around their legs. The air was cold, the sea green as bottle glass. Mr. Scollins was looking a little green, too.

"Doesn't it bother you the way the horizon slides up and down?" he asked.

"I don't notice it," Barry said. "Why

< *80* >

don't you close your eyes?" He looked around. Nice and safe here. Rows of passengers, mummy-wrapped like themselves, were lined up on either side of them . . . Was there really a mummy in the hold below them, lying snugly in its coffin? Some of the passengers walked briskly along the deck, bulked up in heavy overcoats. There always seemed to be deck walkers.

"You think Mrs. Adair really hit her husband?" Scollins asked.

Barry shrugged.

"If you ask me, it's all in the child's imagination," Scollins said, putting the tips of his long fingers together. "Anyone can see the little girl doesn't like her mother. Mrs. Adair is a lady. Did you notice her pearls? They're real, and of excellent quality. They'd probably go for three hundred guineas at least, wholesale."

He pulled his chin deep into his collar. "I may just close my eyes for a while," he told Barry. "I want your word that you won't go roaming off someplace if I sleep."

"I won't," Barry promised. He certainly wasn't going anywhere near the poop deck, not even to look down on it

< 81 >

from a safe distance. Not today or any other day while he was on board.

He lay watching the sparkle of cold sun on cold ocean. No land anywhere. Nothing. What a terrible thing if the ship did sink! Nowhere to swim to. Nothing but emptiness, and your feet going down, feeling for a bottom that wasn't there, and your head going under the waves—down, down into that greenness. Shivers chased one another up and down his legs. What a thing to think about. Howard and he. Two of a kind. The wooden arms of his deck chair throbbed slightly under his hands. The ship must be moving fast, moving him away from Ireland. "There's no turning back now," Mary Kelly had said last night. The words were as final as the priest saying amen.

Once he thought he saw Jonnie Flynn come out of a swinging door halfway along the deck, but it was only someone built like him, someone young, swaggering. Barry relaxed his hold on his knife. He didn't have much to worry about up here in the daytime. The nights were when he'd have to be careful.

The deck steward came pacing toward

< 82 >

him, balancing one of the small silver trays with an engraved White Star emblem. On it was an envelope. *Someone was getting a message delivered from the wireless room,* Barry thought. *Or maybe it's an answer to a message already sent. Maybe something about that stock quotation.* But the deck steward had stopped, holding the tray out. "Mr. Barry O'Neill? Letter for you."

"For me?" It was in a *Titanic* envelope, the kind of embossed stationery they had in the writing-room desks. Barry took it and turned it in his hand.

"Who gave it to you?" he asked.

"It was left on the tray, sir." The deck steward gestured toward the serving cart that held silver teapots, sugars and creamers, cups and saucers.

"And you knew who I was, to bring it to me?" Barry asked.

The steward smiled. "Oh, yes, sir. I know all my passengers."

"Well, thanks." Barry glanced at the sleeping Scollins, then opened the envelope. Inside, on the single sheet of paper it said, "Meet me tonight at ten. Promenade deck." It was signed Pegeen Flynn.

< 83 >

Pegeen Flynn! It was a trick, of course, to get him to a quiet place on the night-dark deck. Maybe she had written and signed the letter, but it had been her brothers' idea. Did they think he was an idiot?

The deck stewards were pushing the serving carts, offering tea and hot cocoa and mugs of steaming Bovril.

I won't go, Barry decided. But what if the Flynn girl wanted to give him Grandpop's glove? He remembered the way she'd looked at him as she'd held it. There'd been a softness about her.

He read the letter again. Beside him

< 84 >

Scollins breathed heavily. His mouth had fallen open and a little spit bubble hung on the corner of his lower lip.

What I should do, Barry thought, *is go right now and check out that deck. I could find something to hide behind and then tonight I could get there early, hide, see if she comes, see if she's alone.*

"Cocoa, sir?"

"No. No, thanks."

"Shall I waken Mr. Scollins?"

"Better not. Just let him sleep." Amazing, they did know all the names.

Maybe he could get Scollins to go with him tonight. Suggest a walk. But Scollins would be useless.

Much later, when Scollins woke complaining that he was half-frozen and asking why everyone around them had empty cups and they'd missed him, Barry suggested a walk on the promenade deck. "It'll get your blood moving," he said.

They walked briskly, to keep their blood from freezing entirely.

There was nothing to see except the wide expanse of deck, the railing, and the stretch of calm, smooth ocean beyond.

< 85 >

There were other promenaders like themselves. But Barry saw nowhere he could hide tonight. Still, there would be nowhere for Jonnie and Frank Flynn to hide either. That was something.

During dinner and afterward, while he and Scollins sat in the first-class reception room listening to the string orchestra, he worried about it. What should he do?

He was in bed before ten, the curtains tightly closed. Was Pegeen Flynn coming up through the ship, coming some secret, hidden way that only the likes of the Flynns would know about? Was she waiting now? Or were all three there waiting, waiting for him?

Stupid to go.

When the idea came he sat up, his heart pounding. *Of course.*

Quickly he pulled on the fisherman's sweater over his pajama top. What was it Grandpop had said about the fishes eating your face off? *Don't think about that.* His long, coarse trousers, the penknife safely in the right-hand pocket. The whistle warm against his chest. His cap and boots. He slid Grandpop's other glove safely

< 86 >

under the pillow. He'd lost the one for the right hand; he would take no chances on losing the other.

Carefully, quietly, he opened the cabin door.

Watley was in the corridor. The night lights gleamed on his polished hair, threw shadows around his sharp little nose. He was natty in his black trousers and white jacket with a bright red flower in the buttonhole. Cradled in his arms was a shoe box, or a box that shape and size. It was the color of a faded leaf, traced with a faint gold design.

"Are you going visiting again tonight, Mr. O'Neill?" he asked.

"No. Just first-class walking."

Watley nodded. "Be careful anyway, sir. The night is dark and we're far from shore."

Barry edged a little away. Watley was being the turbaned fortune-teller again, his lips unmoving. The card coming out of the slot said, *You will cross a body of deep water where danger awaits.*

Barry wet his lips, managed a small laugh. "Well, I'm not in a rowboat, so I'll

< 87 >

try not to worry. What have you got in the box? It looks old . . . interesting."

Watley didn't glance down. "It is both old and interesting. Perhaps I will show you what's inside, Mr. O'Neill, but not tonight.

"No, not tonight."

Barry walked quickly away, resisting the urge to look back and see if Watley was still watching. The cabin steward gave him the creeps. Bad enough that he had to go now and face one of the Flynns, or three of the Flynns, without worrying about Watley.

He took the elevator down to the promenade deck level and waited just inside the swinging exit doors. The great ship surrounded him with warmth and comfort. Music still drifted faintly from the reception room. The band had switched now from operetta to ragtime. Some of the young set would be dancing—Mrs. Cherry Hat, for one. It was the kind of music that made Barry's feet tap. But not tonight.

Someone would come along soon, someone he could walk with, and be safe

< 88 >

with, and inconspicuous. The crystal chandelier in the à la carte restaurant tinkled a soft silver bell of an accompaniment, *ting, ting, ting*.

A lady in a long dark blue evening cape and a man in black tie and tails passed him in a drift of perfume. The woman arched her thin eyebrows and said something to the gentleman. Barry guessed it would be something like, "What's that uncouth-looking character doing up here in first class? Should we report him?"

He waited uneasily. Already the elegant cherub clock said ten minutes past ten. If she had come, would she have waited? Jonnie and Frank would wait forever if they were there.

A young couple warmly dressed for the night air came up the staircase and pushed out onto the deck. Barry let them go. He'd promised himself a group of three, at least.

Then he saw two men and a woman coming up the grand staircase. They were bundled into heavy coats and mufflers. One of the men wore knickers and walking boots. The woman had on one of

< 89 >

those leather caps like flyers' helmets, with flaps that came down over her ears. Barry moved quickly. He pushed open the door, stepped out, and held it for them. Cold bit at him through the oiled wool of his sweater, through the thick tweed of his trousers.

"Bracing night," one of the men said to Barry, and the woman smiled. "A good walk before retiring brings a good night's rest."

"Yes," Barry said. "My grandfather and I used to walk every night when I was home. But he isn't here with me." The words came out more forlorn than he'd intended, and no wonder. The night walks with Grandpop down the Mullinmore Road were too close and too well remembered.

"Walk with us, why don't you?" The woman had the kindest voice. "I'm Mrs. Goldstein. This is my husband, and this is my brother, Arthur." Arthur was the one in the red scarf.

"I'm Barry O'Neill. I'd like to walk with you very much. Thanks."

The deck was empty except for them

< 90 >

and the young couple way ahead. Too cold for most passengers to walk. Certainly too cold to stand around and admire the sweep of the night ocean and the star-filled sky. The deck lights shone yellow, bathing everything in their shivering light. If Pegeen was here he'd see her. If Jonnie and Frank were here . . . well, he'd see them, too. He eased the whistle so the loop of it hung outside the neck of his sweater. He doubted if they'd come at him anyway, not with the Goldsteins and Arthur, all three of them, striding out strong and healthy.

They walked in silence, their footsteps silent, too, on the damp wooden planks of the deck. There was only the swish, swish of the sea below as the *Titanic* sliced through it, only the wind shearing the funnels, keening like a banshee.

So strange to think of the ship gliding on top of all that deep, dark water, moving in the glow of its own lights, spreading the wings of its own white foam. What did the fish think? Forty-five thousand tons of metal and wood, propellers the size of windmills, a rudder as big as a tree. How

< 91 >

did this thing get into their ocean? If you flew above, though, looking down, she'd be no bigger in this immense ocean than a walnut shell in a wide lake.

The young couple had rounded the bow, and there was no one in sight. No one. Had Pegeen been here and gone? Or was it all a trick from the beginning?

Mr. Goldstein pointed up. "See the whiskers around the lights?" he asked.

Barry looked and saw little sparks of color dancing in the air above them.

"Those are splinters of ice caught in the deck lights," Mr. Goldstein said.

"Like bugs around porch lamps at home," Mrs. Goldstein said. "Shiver, shiver." She shook herself under her heavy coat, and the ear flaps on her cap jiggled like a dog's ears, but she was smiling, all white teeth and healthy, cold-whipped cheeks. "Wonderful, isn't it?"

They were nearing the bow themselves now, turning in the shelter of the wide glass panels that shielded them from the wind. The wireless aerials above swung and clicked against the tall mast, and way, way up, the White Star flag whipped and cracked against the brilliant sky.

< 92 >

When they rounded the turn to port side, the wind of the ship's making caught them again and they stopped to get their breath. Mrs. Goldstein wiped her eyes. "Oh, my. That will put a shine on your feathers."

And that was when Barry saw two figures at the rail and one standing back farther along the deck. They were here! All three of them! He'd known it all along.

And then he recognized the couple by the railing. He'd seen them last night, the woman in the pale fur coat; tonight, again, she turned her head away from them as they passed. But tonight she didn't turn it away fast enough, and Barry saw it was Mrs. Adair. He saw the crown of braided fawn-colored hair, the gleam of the pearls at her neck, the pearls that Scollins had admired earlier. Could the man possibly be Peter, little Jocelyn's father? The one Mrs. Adair had whacked on the head? But he was supposed to have been left behind, and these two had been kissing. Barry sensed it even if he hadn't seen it. Was this someone else?

No time to think about it now, though, because there was a girl in a long,

< 93 >

dark coat standing farther along the deck. She stood well back, as if hoping for shadows, but there were no shadows to hide among. No one was with her. There was a door, though, the port twin of the one they'd come through earlier on the starboard side. Two fellows could hurl themselves through that and be on him in a minute.

Barry didn't even glance at her as they passed, though he knew it was Pegeen. Knew, too, that she saw him. She took a small step forward, then back.

When he and the Goldsteins were opposite the door he said, "Thanks for letting me walk with you. I think I've had enough now, and I'll go in."

"Really? Too bad. We're planning on another turn around." Mrs. Goldstein put a gloved hand on his shoulder. "Come walk with us any night. We're in Cabin Two B. Come see us anytime if you're lonely for your grandfather. We miss our two grandsons already. In fact, we're planning another trip to visit them."

Barry nodded. They were so nice. "Lucky grandchildren," he said. He

< 94 >

glanced nervously at the swinging doors. If only he could ask the Goldsteins to come inside with him . . . But how could he do that?

"Good-night, then," they called, moving on.

"Good-night."

He had his whistle between his lips even as they turned; had the door open, the little penknife in his hand. There was no one there. The ship, serene and warm and quiet, hummed around him. He could hear the music, but fainter now. . . .

He circled back, wide, toward Pegeen Flynn, keeping a distance between himself and the railing, looking up, sideways, every way. She was the only one here.

She wore the long, dark coat and the boots he'd seen her in on the dock, but a black shawl hid her hair and shoulders, blowing a little where she didn't hold it.

"I was certain sure the message didn't get to you," she said.

"It did." Barry had trouble keeping his glance on her. The swinging door was in his line of sight if he stood sideways.

She pointed to the whistle. "What's

< 95 >

this?" Then answered herself, "Och, sure, Jonnie and Frank have had a lot of these blown in their faces."

"And they'll have one blown again, and worse, if they come near me," Barry said.

"They'll not be coming near you," Pegeen said. "They're happy enough with themselves for what they already did to you." Her finger, cold as an icicle, touched the stitches in his face and the hurt skin around them.

He jerked his head away. "What they want is to throw me in the ocean."

"They'd never. They're braggarts, the both of them, but they're not bad. Whatever they did in Mullinmore, they had good reason."

"What reason?" Barry asked. He wanted to add "to be thieves," but she was their sister so he didn't say that. Instead he said, "If we're going to keep talking we should go inside before we freeze."

"No. I room with Mary Kelly way below, at the back. She wanted to come with me, for we don't trust you no more than you trust us. I told her I had to come by

< 96 >

myself, because what was done to you was done by my brothers. Here." From under the shawl she took the glove. "You were late getting to me. Mary will be fretting already."

The glove was warm from being under the shawl and close to her body. Barry held it in both hands. "Thanks."

"I saw old Mr. O'Neill give the pair of them to you as the ship was leaving," she said. The wind lifted the tail of her shawl, blew it against him, dropped it again. This close, he could see the shower of freckles across her cheekbones. He saw the tears. "My ma gave me . . . this." Her hand touched a silver brooch at her neck. "It has a bit of her hair inside. I wouldn't want to lose it ever in my life." Her voice choked. "Never mind. You'd have no interest in what my ma gave me. I have to go."

"I would have interest. I'm missing Mullinmore and everything. I don't want to leave either." Why was he saying these things to her? Only because she was from home. Only because she'd given him back the glove . . . "I've never seen you about

< 97 >

the town." Cold froze his face, made him pull his elbows against himself, made him hold himself tight and small so there'd be no gap for its bite to come through.

"I've been away, living with my aunt Maggie. There's too many of us at home, that's why—" She stopped and he saw the small shrug of her shoulders that said again, *What do you care?*

"I have to go," she repeated, and turned.

He caught at the shawl. "Is your cabin all right?" What a dopey question. She'd know it was just to keep her here an extra minute that he'd asked.

He saw her pleased little smile. She knew.

"It's nice enough, but it's awful small. Mary and I gave our life jackets to Jonnie and Frank to store for us. They take up too much room."

"How did you get to this deck any-way?"

Her smile widened. "Jonnie and Frank were telling the others the way if they wanted to come. There's an alley down on E Deck. The sailors call it Scotland Road.

< 98 >

It runs the length of the ship." This time her smile mocked him. "There's a locked gate that's not that hard to go up over." She tugged at the shawl and freed it from his grip. "Now you know. You know how to get down to us if you have a mind for it."

He watched her turn and go. He watched her till the swinging doors closed behind her.

< 99 >

Sometimes Barry dreamed about his mother and father. That night he dreamed they were standing by the railing of the *Titanic,* kissing, and when he came along they pulled apart.

"Mother! Father!" Barry called out in his dream voice, running toward them on dream-light feet. But his mother turned her back and looked out to sea, and his father said, "It's only your mother and father. You wouldn't be interested."

When he wakened it was still dark. The only sound was the throb of the ship's engines. The beat seemed louder, faster, but maybe he thought so because of the night

< *100* >

and the quiet. Scollins turned and murmured sleepily in the other bed.

Barry had Grandpop's gloves, both of them, under his pillow, and he put them on now. The right one seemed still to be warm with the warmth of Pegeen Flynn, but that he was certainly imagining. The warmth had to have come from his own bed.

He wished Pegeen had lived in Mullinmore instead of with her auntie, whoever that was. He and she might have been friends. But probably not. The likes of the O'Neills were not friendly with the likes of the Flynns. He thought of the little unpainted Flynn house in Dead Lane, next to the chapel graveyard. How many rooms did it have? Two, maybe, and a kitchen. How many children were there? Seven or eight, at least. But, but . . . He thought of the way Pegeen's brothers and sisters had clung to her, the wailing heartbreak in Mrs. Flynn's voice when she'd seen her sons and daughter go. She loved them. They loved each other.

He wished Grandpop had never complained about the scratch. But Jonnie

< 101 >

Flynn was headed for trouble. It would have come to him some way.

Barry turned restlessly. If only he could have talked to Pegeen more! He'd like to have known . . . His thoughts were getting hazier and hazier, and the beat of the ship . . . He fell asleep.

When he wakened next it was morning and Watley was in the cabin with the breakfast tea. He brought Barry his cup and saucer. "My word, sir. Were your hands cold in the night? You should have rung for me. I will be sure to put an extra blanket on your bed this evening."

"No," Barry said. "I was quite warm." Embarrassed, he pulled off his gloves and pushed them back under his pillow. Was there nothing that escaped Watley's attention?

"I think I'm feeling a little better this morning," Scollins announced. "I think I will even venture to the dining salon for breakfast."

Barry and he went together. On the other side of the elegant room, Barry saw the Goldsteins, his friends of last night, at

< *102* >

their table. He waved to them. Cabin 2B. He could go and visit them if he wanted to. The thought made him less lonely.

Mrs. Adair and Jocelyn were already seated with Colonel Sapp.

"Morning! Morning!" the colonel said heartily, and Mrs. Adair's eye flick-flicked to Barry and then back to her plate. He knew she'd recognized him when he walked by last night.

"Did the shark come up onto the deck again?" Jocelyn asked him. For the first time she seemed like a normal little girl.

Barry shook his head. "No, I called to him from the rail. I called, 'Sharky, Sharky! Come and take another bite,' but he'd disappeared."

"Probably couldn't keep up with the ship." Colonel Sapp wiped his mustache carefully on his serviette. "I hear the captain is determined to make New York by Tuesday. He's out to beat the *Olympia*'s record. Wouldn't be surprised if there's a bonus in it for him."

"Is that much speed safe?" Mrs. Adair asked.

"Makes no difference, I should think.

< 103 >

The *Titanic* has the strength of fifty thousand horses in her engines, and she's built strong enough to take any speed he fancies. No chance of hitting anything. She'll not meet up with much traffic out here in the North Atlantic."

"There may be icebergs," Barry said.

"Shouldn't be surprised. Be surprised if there weren't, at this time of year." The colonel looked reassuringly at Mrs. Adair. "No need to worry, though, dear lady. There's always a lookout, day and night, in the crow's nest. Those fellows could spot a football in the water a mile away, especially when the sea's this calm."

The sea did seem particularly calm, Barry thought, when he and Mr. Scollins went up after breakfast for a walk on the boat deck.

"I'm happy to be feeling better," Mr. Scollins said. "My whole family has sensitive stomachs." He spoke with satisfaction. "It's a sign of good breeding."

"I'm sure it is," Barry said.

A couple was walking toward them, the woman waving enthusiastically. It was Mrs. Cherry Hat, with her husband,

< 104 >

Howard. They exchanged good mornings, then Mrs. Cherry Hat whispered to Barry, "You'll never guess what Howard's been doing. He's counting lifeboats."

"Whatever for?" Mr. Scollins gave Howard the kind of glance reserved for a four-year-old.

"Oh, he's got this fixation," Howard's wife said in a stage whisper. "It's all because of that ridiculous book, you know, the one he read before we sailed. That ship, the *Titan*, didn't have enough lifeboats. That's why they were all *doomed*."

"This ship doesn't have enough either," Howard said. "Can't understand it." He was looking at Barry. "Could someone please explain to me why there are only sixteen lifeboats on a liner this size?"

"He has counted them every day," his wife said, nodding solemnly. "And the numbers never change."

"There are four toward the bow on this side and another four toward the stern. The same on the port side."

"Perhaps there are others on another deck," Mr. Scollins suggested, frowning.

< 105 >

"No. We've been all over," Howard said.

Mrs. Cherry Hat rolled her eyes. "Indeed, we've been all over."

"There are also four canvas collapsibles," Howard said. "I've multiplied and added till I'm dizzy. According to the posted lists there are two thousand, two hundred and seven people on this ship. All the boats together, filled to capacity, could only carry one thousand, one hundred and seventy-eight. However many times I try, that means no room in the lifeboats for more than a thousand people."

"Howard likes things to add up," his wife said.

"I do like to think everyone would be saved in an emergency."

Barry sensed the rising irritation in Howard's voice. His wife must have sensed it, too.

"You're quite right," she said. "There should be enough lifeboats to carry everyone. You know what, Howard? When we get home we will write to our congressman and to the White Star Line."

"Fine idea." Howard's voice was

< 106 >

frosty. "Let us go, Marjorie. I believe we are already quite late for breakfast."

"The man does have a fixation," Mr. Scollins said when they were out of ear-shot. "However, if what he says is true, we should write to the White Star Line our-selves. Adequate safety precautions never hurt and often help. Mr. Billings and Mr. Fetters are very careful in the shop. We keep a fire extinguisher behind the counter at all times."

Barry nodded. "That's good."

"Speaking of Mr. Fetters, I should check on my bag at the purser's office," Scollins said.

When they'd made sure it was safely locked away, they strolled around the great ship and explored the library, its shelves filled with the classics and all the newest novels, too. Barry borrowed *The Last of the Mohicans,* a novel by James Fenimore Cooper about the American In-dians. He didn't expect to see any Indians in Brooklyn, but it would be good to know something about them and about the land beyond the cities. He and Mr. Scollins looked into the gymnasium,

< 107 >

where passengers were pedaling stationary bicycles or bucking about on leather horses. There was also a swimming pool, a squash court, a Turkish bath with gilded cooling rooms, and a trained masseuse.

"Good heavens! There's everything," Barry said, and he thought, *With all these luxuries they probably didn't have room for more lifeboats.* But he decided it was wise not to bring up the subject of lifeboats again.

It was strange how little he was worrying about Jonnie and Frank Flynn today. Perhaps because Scollins was with him, or because it was daylight with lots of people around, or . . . Pegeen Flynn moved like a shadow in and out of his mind. "They're braggarts, the both of them," she'd said, "but they're not bad. Whatever they did in Mullinmore, they had good reason." *What reason?* he wondered.

This was the afternoon the doctor was supposed to look at his stitches. He went up to the infirmary and afterward to the Marconi Room again. The first rush was over, so today it wasn't so crowded. Barry filled in one of the wireless forms. "Mr.

< *108* >

and Mrs. Flynn, Dead Lane, Mullinmore, County Cork," he printed. "Everything all right. Having a wonderful trip. Signed, Jonnie, Frank, and Pegeen." There! It would be his secret gift to her. A way of saying thank you for returning his glove. Her mother might tell her sometime in a letter about how she'd been delivered this message, and how much better it made her feel, and Pegeen would wonder and then maybe she'd smile, knowing.

The wireless operator was still busy, tapping out his messages, his earplugs on. But the second operator, Bride, seemed ready for a chat. He counted the words, and Barry counted out his money. "Are you Jonnie or Frank?" Bride asked. "I know you're not Pegeen."

"No, she's prettier than I am," Barry said, and wondered, *Is she pretty? I expect so.* He remembered her eyes, the same green as the sea; flecks in them, too, brown flecks. He shook his head, embarrassed, though certainly the operator couldn't read his mind the way he could read the tapped-out wireless messages.

"Any more word about icebergs?"

< 109 >

Barry asked. "Last time I was here there were some warnings."

Bride jerked his head back toward the first operator. "Sparks is sick to death of those iceberg warnings. They're jamming the airwaves, and we have a backlog of passengers' messages to get out."

"You mean other ships are sending messages about icebergs?" Barry asked.

"They are. 'Surrounded by ice.' 'Stuck in ice.' Sparks just got through to Cape Race, and these silly messages keep interrupting. Of course there's ice. We know that. We don't need them to tell us every half hour."

He pulled the form off the pad. "I can't promise to get this out right away, but we'll send it as soon as we can."

"Thanks," Barry told him.

He'd dawdled so long that there was hardly time to change for dinner, but he made it with minutes to spare. Afterward he and Scollins went to the lounge to watch and hear Gilbert and Sullivan's *HMS Pinafore*. ". . . I am the monarch of the sea, the ruler of the queen's na-vee . . ." *Yes,* Barry thought. *Just the way Captain Smith was the ruler of the* Titanic.

< *110* >

Scollins suggested an early night. "I haven't been sleeping well at all," he said. "We've had an energetic day, Mr. O'Neill, and you have your book. The cabin light will not disturb me. I'd appreciate it if we could retire early. Frankly, I'm not happy to have you wandering the ship without me."

Barry didn't want to wander on his own either, but it was too early to go to bed. "I'll hang about for a while," he told Scollins, "but I won't be long."

He considered going to the Goldsteins' room to ask if he could walk with them, but it was very cold now, even colder than last night. He decided he'd just take a peek outside, then join Scollins in their cabin. *The Last of the Mohicans* and a warm bed did sound inviting.

He opened the swing doors and felt the air sting his face, saw the dazzling whiskers of ice doing their colored dance around the deck lights. He noticed, too, a small crowd of passengers clustered about the railing, looking down.

"Oh!" one of them said. "Look! How beautiful."

What was going on?

< *111* >

"It's an itty-bitty iceberg," a young woman called to him. "Come and see. It's so pretty."

She stood aside so he could take her place by the railing. "It's a baby one," someone said.

The berg was no bigger than a good-sized boulder, floating and turning gently in the ripples that spread from the *Titanic*'s bow. Under the stars it gleamed smooth as silk, a shiny, silvery blue.

"I bet you could see yourself in it," a woman said.

"Mermaids' looking glass," a man told her. "In fact, I think I just saw a mermaid over on the other side, combing her hair."

The little berg was being left behind now as the *Titanic* glided on.

"See who sees another iceberg first," someone suggested. But there wasn't another one to be seen in the whole wide width of the ocean, and the group broke up, shivering. Someone said, "Let's go dance. Roger's promised to show us the steps to the hootchy-kootch. It's all the rage."

Barry was glad to get inside, too. He wasn't dressed for this kind of cold. He

< 112 >

thought about the ice and the ice warnings. No one seemed to be worried,
though, and there were those lookouts
way up in the crow's nest. He wasn't going to worry either.

He took the elevator down and was almost at the cabin when he saw Watley.

"Good evening, sir." Watley made his
strange little jerky bow. "You're retiring
early?

"I am. It's too cold to be out, and I
have a good book."

"I was hoping to have a word with you
and Mr. Scollins, sir. I just brought him a
brandy and milk. Would now be con-
venient?"

"Of course," Barry said, and he let
Watley knock and then open the door to
Scollins's irritable "Come in."

Scollins was sitting up in bed reading
a pamphlet called "Rubies, Diamonds,
and Other Gems." The glass that had held
his brandy and hot milk was on the little
bedside table, only a white rim of froth
along the top to show it had once been
full.

Watley stood in the middle of the

< 113 >

cabin. "Gentlemen, I know this is a nuisance, but you are my passengers and in my charge. I have only eight cabins under my care, and I take a special responsibility for all of you."

"Yes, yes." Scollins finger-marked his place in the pamphlet.

"As you know, this is my first trip on the *Titanic*." Watley smiled his tight-lipped smile. "That goes without saying. It appears there is not to be a lifeboat drill. The ship is, after all, unsinkable. But I am accustomed to making certain that my passengers know how to put on their life jackets and how to proceed to their correct boat stations." He paused.

So strange, the way shadows moved and spread across Watley's face, like clouds across a summer sky. It must be because of where he stood and the angle of the two cabin lights, Barry decided. And the movement of the ship, of course.

"And so?" Scollins swung his legs out of bed and sat dangling them, his feet sticking out long and white from the bottoms of his striped pajamas. "I appreciate your attitude, Watley. Carry on."

< 114 >

"Thank you, sir. So far this has been a calm crossing, and of course we do not foresee an emergency. Nevertheless . . ."

Watley pulled fat white life jackets from the shelves in the wardrobes, showed Barry and Scollins how to put their arms through the canvas tapes and pull the buckles tight in front. "Uncomfortable, I know," he said. "But should anything untoward occur, these will keep you afloat indefinitely."

The life jacket was rough under Barry's chin. He could hardly see or move around the bulk of it. He had a quick flash of Mary Kelly's brother dancing with Pegeen, the canvas tapes and buckles swinging around them. "He can't swim. He's going to keep it on until we get to New York," Mary Kelly had said. Was he really going to wear one of these for all that time?

Watley helped them take the life jackets off and stored them away. "Your nearest lifeboat station would be on the boat deck, starboard side. Should there be"—he paused—"a dangerous situation, put your life jackets on immediately and

< 115 >

proceed there as quickly as possible. I will of course be here to assist you. Thank you, gentlemen."

"Thank you." Scollins smiled a warm smile. While Watley was within hearing he said, "I think that fellow deserves a special letter to the White Star Line. He certainly is conscientious."

Watley closed the door quietly, and Barry opened it again after him. "May I speak to you for a minute, Watley?"

"Certainly, sir." Watley stood motionless. "You have a problem, Mr. O'Neill?"

"It's just . . ." Barry didn't know how to put it. "I keep hearing about ice and icebergs. And you—well, it's almost as if you know something, which I realize seems ridiculous, but . . ."

Watley's eyes were glazed, as though covered with transparent paper. "What could I know, sir?"

"I have no idea. It's . . . well, you said it yourself. The sea is big and our ship is small. I'd like to know . . ."

For a second the eye glaze seemed to lift. "Yes." It was almost as if Watley had come to some kind of decision. "Follow

< 116 >

me if you will, Mr. O'Neill. I think now is the time to show you."

Barry walked behind him down the corridor to a door marked Cabin Steward. Watley opened it with a key that he took from his pocket and stood aside for Barry.

The cabin was not as luxurious as theirs, but it was comfortable. A narrow bed, a dresser, and a table that hinged down from the wall. On the dresser beside a tortoiseshell brush-and-comb set was the faded green box.

"Please sit down, Mr. O'Neill."

Barry sat on the straight-backed chair by the small mahogany table.

Watley set the box on the table's shining surface and lifted the lid. Inside was something that looked like old crumpled paper. He lifted it out, letting it droop, shapeless, between his fingers. It was as long as a baby's dress.

"I wanted to show you this," he said.

"What is it?" Barry felt a chill deep in his stomach. He put his hands behind his back and felt himself strain away from whatever it was Watley held.

"It's a caul. I was born in it. A child

< 117 >

born in a caul will have the gift and the curse of seeing what you cannot." He spoke in his fortune-teller voice again, toneless but with something of the Irish in it—the western islands, maybe; Achill or Aran or farther out. The light from the brass wall lamp gleamed on the caul, on the onionskin fineness of it, its spider-spun gloss. Those strange shadows chased themselves across Watley's face.

"I see disaster," he said.

< 118 >

CHAPTER 8

"Disaster? Do you mean for me? Myself?" Barry asked. The picture of him, himself, somersaulting over the railing into the dark ocean was terrifying. "You don't mean disaster for the ship, do you? It can't sink. You can't mean that."

But Watley simply floated the shimmer of caul back into its box, closed the lid, and said, "I'm sure I can't say, sir."

Couldn't or wouldn't?

All night long Barry thought about the caul, about the ice warnings in the Marconi Room, about Howard saying there weren't enough lifeboats. "We're all doomed," Howard had said, but *doomed*

was the word used about the *Titan,* not the *Titanic.*

Sometime just before first light filtered through the window, carrying the reflection of the predawn sea, Barry sat straight up in his bunk. The words Pegeen Flynn had tossed at him, the words pounced on by the wind as they talked, jumped back into his mind: "It's nice enough, but it's awful small." She'd been talking about the cabin. "Mary and I gave our life jackets to Jonnie and Frank to store for us. They take up too much room."

She'd said that. She had. He must warn her.

Sunday morning, and church services for the first-class passengers were in the lounge. Around Barry the congregation sang: "Eternal father strong to save . . . " Beside him Scollins bellowed the hymn. Scollins had the worst voice—like a rook's it was—and the squawk of it was louder than anybody's.

Barry had to get to Pegeen and Mary fast, because who knew when this disaster might happen? He could go to steerage

< 120 >

himself. He knew women were at the back of the ship, but he had no idea which cabin was Pegeen's and how to find it. What would he say?—"The ship might sink. Go right away and get your life jackets from Jonnie and Frank?"

He imagined Pegeen's flashing green eyes. "Och, don't be daft. Don't you know this is the *Titanic?*"

Around him the voices rose in praise, heedless of what they sang:

> *O hear us when we cry to thee*
> *For those in peril on the sea.*

Nobody with a thought that they might be in peril. Except Watley, of course. And Watley might have meant that only Barry was in danger. From the Flynns. He had looked half crazy anyway, holding up that caul. Who would believe Watley any more than they'd believe the turbaned fortune-teller at the fair? Nobody but superstitious Barry, and maybe superstitious Howard. But still, he wished Pegeen had her life jacket.

Barry's skin was clammy under his shirt. He eased a finger around the collar,

< 121 >

felt the chain that held the whistle move slightly, cool and smooth against his stillness. He looked at the shining Sunday faces. There were Colonel Sapp and Mrs. Adair and little Jocelyn, Howard and Mrs. Cherry Hat. She saw him looking and gave him a cheeky wink. Mr. and Mrs. Goldstein and Arthur weren't here. They were probably Jewish and would have been at Jewish services yesterday. He saw the Ryersons and Henry Sleeper Harper up in the front row. All these people. If anything happened . . .

Captain Smith, very dignified in his uniform, finished his reading from the Book of Psalms.

Barry shivered. *Suppose I leapt up and ran to the front and shouted, "Everybody listen. The ship is going to sink. Make the captain turn back"?* But they were as far from one shore as the other. The passengers would think he was dotty. Scollins would die of acute mortification. And so would he.

The service was over now and Captain Smith was leaving. In a minute he'd be gone.

< 122 >

Barry pushed quickly past the people between himself and the space that had been left in the middle of the rows of chairs.

"Excuse me. Excuse me."

Behind him Scollins whispered loudly, "What are you doing? Just where do you think you're—"

Barry planted himself in front of the captain so the man couldn't get past. "Captain Smith."

"Yes?" Hands clasped behind him, a kindly smile on his bearded face, the captain leaned toward Barry.

"I . . . I need to ask you something. Are we in any danger from icebergs?"

The eyebrows beetled. The smile faded a little. Captain Smith rocked back and forth on his feet, the way a man would who was accustomed to standing on a heaving bridge in a stormy sea. "Are you frightened, my boy?" he asked, peering more closely. "Oh, yes, you and I have met before. Did our ship's doctor take good care of your wound?"

"Yes, sir. Thank you. It's fine."

Mr. Scollins was beside Barry now,

< 123 >

taking his elbow, frowning apologetically at the captain. "Captain Smith."

The captain stopped Scollins with a wave of his hand. "Are you traveling alone, son?" he asked Barry.

Barry nodded toward Scollins. "Except for Mr. Scollins. I mean, no one in my family is with me."

"I'm so—" Scollins began.

The captain stopped him again in mid-sentence. "Mr. Collins."

"Scollins. It's an Anglo-Saxon name. I believe there was a Scollins who fought with King Henry at Agincourt. My mother always—"

"Quite so." Captain Smith stroked his beard and rocked closer to Barry. "Tell you what, old chap. How would you like to see the way the greatest ship in the world is really run? A view from the inside, so to speak."

"I'd like that very much," Barry said.

"Come up on the bridge after the mid-day meal, then. I think I can allay your fears about icebergs and anything else that may be worrying you." He gave Barry a grandfatherly pat on the shoulder and strode away.

< 124 >

"My word." Scollins was beaming, as were all the passengers around them who'd heard the exchange.

"I say, put me in your pocket, old man, will you?" a gentleman in an old Etonian tie said. "The bridge is quite an honor."

"So lovely of the captain," his lady companion murmured. "I do like men who are thoughtful of young people."

Howard pushed up beside them. "Take a good look around," he told Barry. "Ask him about the lifeboats, and his speed."

"I will." He'd ask, too, if there were other collapsibles that Howard had missed on his lifeboat inspection.

It was during the midday meal that Barry got the idea.

"Shall we freshen up before we go to the bridge?" Scollins asked as they walked from the dining salon.

"You go," Barry said. "I have something to do first. I'll be down in a few minutes."

He went quickly before Scollins could argue or question.

In the writing room he took a sheet of *Titanic* paper and wrote, "Meet me, same

< 125 >

place, same time, tonight. Urgent," signed it, and put it in an envelope. "Miss Pegeen Flynn," he printed. It made him smile to think they were becoming pen pals even though they didn't know each other.

Watley was hovering in the corridor outside their cabin. "I understand you are to have a visit with the captain," he said.

News gets around fast, Barry thought. Even on a ship the size of the *Titanic*.

"I trust all confidences will remain, as it were, between us," Watley went on.

He meant his talk of a disaster, of course. "I won't say anything." Barry held out the envelope. "But I need to ask you to do something for me. Can you deliver this? It's for a steerage passenger. She's in a cabin at the stern of the ship."

"Very good, sir. I will give it to her cabin stewardess to place in her room. Is there anything else, Mr. O'Neill?"

"Yes," Barry said. "I've been wondering. Why did you tell me what you told me last night? Why did you show me what you showed me?"

"I have a responsibility to my passengers. Only that, sir."

< 126 >

"So you said. But did you show and tell everything to all your passengers?"

"No, sir. One senses receptiveness."

"I see." What on earth did he mean by that? That Barry was the only one around who was easily terrified?

"I knew you would believe me," Watley said.

The glaze seemed to cover his eyes again, making it hard to look into them, distracting Barry from what he said.

"I will deliver the letter now." Watley gave his little bob of a bow. "If you will excuse me."

"Thanks." Barry watched him glide away down the corridor, his feet in their pointed shoes making no sound on the carpeting.

Scollins came through the cabin door. His hair was slicked down and his face shone with a soap-and-water shine. Oley Palm soap, exclusive to the *Titanic*. "We'd better hurry," Scollins warned.

Barry combed his own hair with his fingers. "I'm ready," he said.

They went up on the elevator, along the deck, unhooked the chain that said No

< 127 >

Entrance—Crew Only, and climbed the steps to the bridge.

"Good afternoon."

"Good afternoon, and welcome." The captain swept his hand expansively around the bridge. "Here we are, gentlemen. The bridge of the RMS *Titanic.*"

It was all glass, like a high, high room made of windows. In front of them was the foredeck, the bow of the ship, and then nothing all around but sea. Looking out and across it, Barry felt they could be the only ones on the ocean. The only ones on the face of the earth.

The ocean today was the dark deep blue of Grandmother's silk Sunday dress. It was as flat as a skating pond and it seemed to stretch forever. There was nothing on it to break the smoothness—no wave, no ripple, no shadow, no hint of land. *I am the monarch of the sea . . .*

A sailor stood by a wheel as big and spoked as a cartwheel, but no cartwheel had ever been this smooth and polished. The sailor's eyes were fixed on the horizon, fixed on nothingness. The black arrow on the compass was steady and unwavering. There was a panel of instru-

< 128 >

ments, a fixed table with colored charts. Another seaman stared through binoculars, turning himself and them in all directions.

The captain shaded his eyes with his hands. "See any icebergs?" he asked, and laughed a gruff bark of a laugh.

"Not right now," Barry said.

"And up there, way up there . . ." The captain stretched back his head and stared upward, as though he could see through the roof of the bridge to the crow's nest. "Up there in the lookout are two of my best men. You've heard of sharpshooters in the Wild West? Those are sharp spotters. We call them the eyes of the ship. If there's anything to see they send down the signal to me."

"And the sharp spotters have binoculars, too, I expect?" Scollins said, nodding wisely.

There was a second's pause, then the captain said, "Actually, no, Mr. Collins. Not on this trip." And Barry sensed a cooling of the friendliness. Wrong question, but smart of Scollins to have asked it.

"We do have binoculars, but somehow

< 129 >

we didn't have enough for everyone, so the bridge took them. We'll pick up more when we get to New York so they can have some in the crow's nest. Believe me, though, they can see perfectly well up there without them. In fact, most of the time lookouts don't bother to use them."

"Yes, I understand. Bit of a nuisance, probably." Scollins was ready to agree to anything.

"We were wondering about lifeboats," Barry said. "One of the passengers thought there might not be enough if there should be an emergency."

"We are fully equipped with lifeboats and meet all current Board of Trade standards," the captain said stiffly. "Besides, what sort of emergency could there be?"

They followed where he pointed, to a panel with rows of buttons on it. "Do you know what this is?"

Barry shook his head.

"With this mechanism I can activate the watertight doors between the bulkheads. I can do it with the touch of a finger. Of course, they can be closed manually as well, from down below.

< 130 >

Also . . ." He paused for effect. "The mechanism is so sensitive that if there is water on the floor in any one of the bulkheads the door will sense it and activate itself. It comes down like a hatchet chop—like a guillotine falling. Not that you've probably ever seen a guillotine fall." He laughed his hoarse laugh. "There are sixteen watertight compartments. Count the buttons."

Barry counted. *I'm like Howard counting lifeboats,* he thought.

"Any two compartments could be flooded and the vessel would still stay afloat," the captain said. "And we would never let two compartments be flooded. This ship won't sink."

"Well," Scollins said, "I certainly feel safe."

"Now, I have a ship to run," Captain Smith said. "Thank you for coming up to admire the wonders of our great liner."

"Thank *you*," Barry said.

He and Scollins went back the way they had come.

"What a marvel of human ingenuity," Scollins said. "When we get to New York

< 131 >

I shall write of this in detail to Mr. Billings and Mr. Fetters. They will be most interested."

Barry was thinking about the letter he'd written to Pegeen Flynn. "Urgent," he'd said. And he was going to warn her about the *Titanic* and the icebergs. He'd planned on telling her what Watley had said if she came. Now he'd feel like a fool. Who with any sense would believe crazy Watley and not Captain Smith?

And come to think of it, why hadn't he just sent her a direct message, to the point, and not vague and mysterious like that? Watley was vague and mysterious enough for all of them. Barry could have said, "It is important that you have your own life jackets in your cabin. For your safety I suggest you get them back from your brothers."

He hadn't done that, and he knew why. The life jackets had given him a reason to talk with her again. The word "urgent" was to force her to come. No use lying to himself. He wanted to see her again.

< 132 >

It was past eleven o'clock. Barry had been around the deck twice, and he knew she wasn't coming. Maybe her brothers had stopped her. Or maybe she'd made the decision herself. Well, it was fine with him.

The letter had been delivered. He knew that.

"I watched personally while the stewardess opened the young lady's door and placed it on her bed," Watley had said.

The night was colder than anything Barry had ever felt. Each time he breathed, his chest hurt way down where the air reached. His nose was numb and dripping, too.

< 133 >

Past eleven, and she wasn't coming. She didn't know how important it was. Well, there was nothing he could do—except maybe he could go find her cabin, find her . . . Someone might see him, though. If he was caught there'd be a terrible commotion about it. A young man from first class going to a young lady's cabin in the middle of the night? And her being in third class would make it worse.

I don't care. I'll go anyway, he thought. *I'll look for that stewardess Watley saw and I'll tell her Pegeen and Mary don't have their life jackets. She probably has spares. I won't try to talk to them,* he thought. Nobody could fault him for that.

He rode the elevator down as far as it went, to B Deck, then took the stairs. Deck G was where the third-class cabins were, Watley had said. The gates across were closed and hung with No Admittance signs, but they weren't locked. At G Deck he turned toward the stern, passing the tightly shut cabin doors that lined the corridor.

There was a different feeling down here. No carpeting, no palm trees in pots, no rich, hushed silence. The engine noise

< 134 >

was steady and there was the sound of the ocean, too. Barry could feel it pushing against the hull. They'd be well under the waterline here. What was keeping the sea out? He sensed it forcing itself against the steel plates: *Let me in. Let me in.* Stop that, he said to himself, fighting the urge to run, to get up and out into the cold, clean air. *The greatest shipbuilders in the world built this,* he told himself. *Irish ship-builders at that.* Everything was perfectly thought out. The strength of the steel, the water pressure per square inch.

Now he was acting like Howard, mul-tiplying in his mind. *Don't think about Howard either. Keep going.*

There was a nice newness to every-thing, though. When the ship was old it might be dingy down here, but now it shone with fresh paint, bright and clean. The poop deck should be directly above him now. Tonight there was no sound of music—too cold outside. Your fingers would freeze on the accordion keys. Your lips would stick to the mouth organ.

Twenty-one G, Twenty-two G, Twenty-three. Which cabin was hers?

"Good evening, sir." A voice as frosty

< *135* >

as the air outside. "Are you looking for something?" The stewardess wore a black dress, a white apron and cap. On the band of her apron was a pin that said Thelma Acheson, Stewardess.

The dragon at the gates protecting the virgins within, Barry thought, remembering school mythology class. "I was looking to find you," he said, sounding even to himself as Irish as a Ballintoy pig. He smiled what he hoped was an innocent smile. "I was talking to Miss Flynn and Miss Kelly earlier. Miss Flynn told me there are no life jackets in their cabin and I began to think how dangerous—"

"No life jackets? Of course there are life jackets. Every cabin has life jackets."

"Well, you see, Miss Acheson, I think they gave them—"

He stopped. There was the sound of loud voices coming closer somewhere around the bend in the corridor. Laughter. A man's voice singing: *"We're off to Philadelphia in the morning."*

"I was about to tell you Miss Flynn and Miss Kelly are not in their cabin," the stewardess said, sounding more dragonlike

< 136 >

than ever. "They were meeting some of their male friends in the third-class lounge." She made the words "male friends" sound sinful. "There's horse racing up there, and dancing, too, I understand. You didn't go yourself?" He felt her grudging approval at that. "I think this might be them returning."

Barry stood beside her, waiting. Pegeen's brothers would be with her, no doubt about that. But who else?

As if on cue, he heard Jonnie Flynn's voice. "Sure, I told you to bet on Killarney Kiss. It was a natural. You're no judge of horseflesh at all, Mick Kelly."

"Horseflesh? Them ould horses are made of wood, and sure they only move to the throw of the dice. I thought Columbus would be a certain winner for us, seeing as how we're doing what he did, in a manner of speaking."

Barry had the glove off his right hand and his fingers curled around the knife in his pocket. He'd put a muffler on over his pullover before he left his cabin, and the whistle hung outside his clothes, hidden by the muffler's trailing ends. He wouldn't

< 137 >

need either it or the knife, he didn't think. Not down here. Not with the dragon lady. But these were the fighting Flynns, and you could never be sure.

The noisy group came around the corner and into the stretch of the corridor. Seven of them, Barry counted, all jumbled together: Pegeen Flynn, her hair fire red in the dim corridor lights, Mary Kelly, Jonnie, Frank, Mary Kelly's brother, Mick, and two other fellows, one big as a horse himself, one puny. Mick Kelly still wore the padded white life jacket.

They stopped and Miss Thelma Acheson moved toward them. Barry saw Frank nudge Jonnie. Saw a few muttered words exchanged, and knew he'd been spotted.

"Be quiet," Miss Acheson whispered in a whisper loud enough to wake the dead and buried. "Have you no thought for the passengers who are sleeping? And what are you boys doing in this part of the ship? You know very well that male visitors are not allowed."

"Och, sure, my darlin', we couldn't let the young ladies go home alone, could we?" That was Mick Kelly. "We're only

< 138 >

walkin' them as far as their cabin doors. Our mothers told us it was polite to go that far and no further."

"And what about him? Mr. Bloody O'Neill from first class?" That was Jonnie Flynn shouting, pushing Mick aside, jutting his chin out at Barry. "What are you doing down here, Mr. Bloody O'Neill?"

"He came to—," the stewardess began. But Jonnie and Frank shouldered her aside.

"Don't you start making trouble here," she said fiercely, and other cabin doors opened, faces peered out, voices called, "What's going on? Where's the trouble?"

The Flynn brothers were in front of Barry. "Sniffing after our sister, were you?" Jonnie Flynn asked. He rubbed the back of his hand hard against the healing stitches in Barry's face, and Barry pulled his head back fast at the needle sting of the stitches' ends pricking into his flesh.

"I told you he had a wild notion of her," Frank Flynn said. "I told you." There was a red gypsy handkerchief knotted at the neck of his ravelly pullover, and

< 139 >

his hands were all big, raw knuckles, opening and closing, ready for use.

"I came to speak to Pegeen and Mary," Barry said. "I tried to send your sister a message but I don't know if she got it."

"You did *what?*" Frank Flynn's face was as red as his handkerchief.

"She didn't get it." That was Mary Kelly. "I did." She took a step closer to Pegeen. "It was there on your bed, Peggy. The stewardess"—she nodded toward Miss Acheson—"I asked her." Mary's voice stumbled as she talked too fast. "She said a steward from first class brought it down. She said it was from a Mr. O'Neill. Oh, Peggy, Peggy. I knew he'd want to see you again. I knew it. And you all starry-eyed over him, and him one of the O'Neills of Mullinmore. And that's the same whether he's here or in America. He's not one of us." She was pleading now, rubbing one of Pegeen's arms. "Remember the maid up at Randalls', at the Big House? Remember how the Randall boy came after her and—"

"So Mr. O'Neill was writing to our

< *140* >

sister, was he? I'll give him writing." Jonnie Flynn leapt forward, but Mick Kelly grabbed him and pulled his head back against the wadding of his white life jacket.

"Easy, man," he said. "We're not needing another fight."

Jonnie was stopped but Frank wasn't. He jabbed one of his big-knuckled fists at Barry, and Barry dodged, the fist thumping against the wall behind him. No need for the knife here. One on one, or two on one—he could handle it. Down here he could. He clenched his teeth. "Come on," he said, putting up his own fists. "Come on."

But Miss Thelma Acheson was between them. Her arms held them apart as easily as Bowers would have held two fighting dogs, one from the other. "You'll stop it now. You!" This was to Barry. "Coming down here and starting trouble! And you!" This to Frank Flynn. "Spoiling for a fight, so you are. I know your kind."

"Please." Pegeen's face was white and angry, the freckles standing out against the paleness. "Am I to understand this, Mary

< 141 >

Kelly? You took and read something that was meant for me?"

"I didn't read it. I took it, that's true. But I never read a word."

Pegeen held out her hand. "Give it to me." Not once had she looked at Barry. Not once.

"It's under my pillow. I was going to give it to you when we were safely landed."

"You did the right thing, Mary girl," Jonnie Flynn said. "You give it to Frank and me, not to her at all."

The stewardess interrupted. "The important question is, Where are the young ladies' life jackets? It is a serious offense to remove life jackets from a cabin."

"We gave them to Jonnie and Frank," Pegeen began guiltily.

"This is not permitted. Who has the life jackets?"

Frank Flynn elbowed his brother. "The O'Neill fellow was that worried about our sister he had to come down here himself in person."

"Too bad him and his didn't worry about us back in Mullinmore. There

< 142 >

wouldn't be a Flynn here if it wasn't for him and his kind, always whining about— no, lamenting—if we looked sideways at them."

"You did a lot more than look sideways," Barry began.

A cabin door opened and an angry voice shouted, "Are you going to gab all night? Will you let a woman get her sleep?"

"Exactly," Miss Acheson said. "You two young ladies go in your cabin. Mr. O'Neill, leave. You others go, and return with Miss Flynn's and Miss Kelly's life jackets. Give them to me."

For the first time Pegeen looked at Barry. Her black dress had the square silver brooch at the high neck and her fingers nervously traced and retraced its outline. "The message? It was to tell me about the life jackets? That was the holy all of it?"

Barry bit his lip. He looked quickly around at the half circle of glowering faces. "There was something else," he said.

"Oh, he's the fly one. 'There was something else,' " Jonnie Flynn said in a

< 143 >

mincing English voice. "Telling her he loved her, likely. Oh, the boyo has the nerve of Brian Boru, so he does."

"Get the letter, Pegeen, and give it to us," Frank said.

"Frank Flynn!" Pegeen's voice was as angry as the brothers'. "Don't tell me what to do. I'm my own person, I am."

"I'm telling yez all to shut up," someone else shouted from farther along the corridor. An angry thump on a cabin wall.

"I'm not going to say it again," Miss Acheson ordered. "Go."

"Aye, go!" the cabin voice shouted.

Miss Acheson pushed them. "Go."

"Don't be letting him near her, then!" Jonnie Flynn shouted back over his shoulder. "I'm putting you in charge. You keep him away from her, or the captain will hear about it."

Mary had her hand on the cabin doorknob. "Twenty-nine G," Barry read. He was glad he knew, and not sure why he was glad.

"I'll read the letter," Pegeen said, looking right at him, and then she was gone.

< 144 >

"Good-night, Mr. O'Neill," the stewardess said firmly.

"Good-night."

Barry went back the way he had come, the knife ready in his pocket, the whistle dangling where he could reach it in a second. It would be hard for them to throw him overboard from here. They'd have to carry him up like an old sack of coal, but they could jump him, the whole holy bunch of them. They could be waiting.

< 145 >

And they were. He heard their breathing before he saw them bunched around the corner at the bottom of the stairs.

"Get him, boys!" Jonnie Flynn shouted.

One on one, or two on one, he might have had a chance, but not five on one; and the boy big as a horse had something in his hand . . . A water carafe? A lemonade bottle? There was no time to see. They were lunging toward him.

Barry pulled the whistle from under his scarf and blew with all his breath. The high, shrill scream of it almost took his head off.

< 146 >

Doors opened everywhere. Voices called. He thought one of the voices belonged to Miss Thelma Acheson.

In a daze of sound and confusion he saw the Flynns and their friends stumbling over each other and running along the corridor, their hands clasped to their ears. And he was running himself, racing up the stairs, the whistle jumping against him at every step, running hard.

He stood by the swing doors that led out to the deck, panting, his whole body wet with sweat. So close. They'd have left him battered and bloody. Would they come looking for him again tonight? He didn't think so. They'd picture him hiding in his cabin. They'd picture how they'd get him another time, when he wasn't ready. Well, there wouldn't be a time when he wasn't ready.

And what about Pegeen? She'd have read the letter by now. Would she come? What had Mary Kelly meant, "And you all starry-eyed over him?" What did that mean?

The door beside him rattled and swung open. Someone was coming in

< 147 >

from the deck. Pegeen? No, she'd never dare step inside here. The dim, deserted first-class deck was one thing, but the gleaming luxury of first class proper would be unthinkable. He stepped back.

Mrs. Adair came through the door; and behind her, holding it open, was the man Barry had seen her with twice before. She wore a pale fur coat. A pale, silky scarf patterned all over with yellow roses was tied around her head. She was half turned, speaking back to the man, and she hadn't yet noticed Barry. He wished there were somewhere he could disappear to and not be standing here with his two arms the one length, but there was nowhere for him to go. Mrs. Adair was smiling. She looked almost happy. Her smile wavered when she saw him.

"Mrs. Adair," Barry said. "Hello." And to the man behind her he said, "Good evening, sir."

"Good evening." The man wore a black homburg hat and a black melton coat with the collar turned up.

"Barry?" Mrs. Adair bit her lip. Her eye began flicking in that horrible, hurtful-looking way.

< 148 >

The man held out his hand. "Barry, we haven't met officially. Charity has told me how nice you are to little Jocelyn."

"Well," Barry said. "It's not hard."

"No." The man removed his hat and turned down the collar of his coat. "It's very cold out there tonight. We took a few steps and decided to come back inside." Under the light of the chandelier his hair shone silver and black. "Charity and I are on our way for a hot drink in the Café Parisien room. Would you care to join us? I hear they have wonderful cinnamon cocoa." His accent was American.

"The stewardess stays with Jocelyn sometimes while I come up with Malcolm," Mrs. Adair said quickly, as if she needed to explain. She pushed back a strand of pale hair that had escaped the scarf. The painted roses were the same as the ones Grandmother grew in her garden, Barry thought, but bigger and brighter. Grandmother's were always a bit sickly and got chewed up by mites.

"Excuse me," Mrs. Adair said. "I should have introduced you. This is my fiancé, Mr. Malcolm Bensonhurst. Mr. Barry O'Neill. Together we suffer the

< 149 >

colonel's stories of his many adventures." She made a face at Barry. "Malcolm came with me to get Jocelyn from her father," she said. "But in the end we decided . . ." She paused.

Mr. Bensonhurst finished the sentence for her. "We decided not to produce me just yet. Charity feels, and I agree, that Jocelyn should be introduced gradually to her new life."

Barry nodded. "She misses her father a lot." The second the words were out he wished them back. What an awful thing to say to Mrs. Adair. To them.

"Yes, she does." Mrs. Adair's eyelid flick, flick, flicked.

Mr. Bensonhurst put a gentle hand on her arm. "Jossie is too young to understand," he said, "and perhaps that is as it should be. The courts awarded her to Charity. Charity's ex-husband took Jossie, though—"

Mrs. Adair put a finger to her lips. "Let's not burden Barry with our troubles."

"It took Charity four years to find her daughter. She literally had to hit Mr. Adair

< 150 >

on the head to free Jocelyn and get her away from him."

"Barry knows a little about that," Mrs. Adair said. "It's hard, Barry, because Jossie doesn't know me." She shivered. "I'm sorry. I've said too much. Forgive me—" In the silence Barry heard the faint tinkle of the crystals that sparkled on the chandelier, the faraway laughter of someone below. Music drifted. Music always drifted from somewhere on the *Titanic,* music and perfume.

"It will be all right, sweetheart," Mr. Bensonhurst said. "Jocelyn will love you. How could she not, when you love her so much? This bad time will pass."

"Yes," Barry said, and the thought of his own mother came like the jab of a knife. "I know it will be hard for you," his mother had said in her last letter, "but we love you so much and we want you with us."

"Yes," he said again. "It will be all right."

Mrs. Adair's smile was warm, her eyes steady. "Thank you. You know, you could have had two cups of that cinnamon cocoa

< 151 >

while we kept you here, talking." She put up a hand and touched his cheek. "Is this a new bruise on your face? How on earth did you get another one?"

"Really?" Barry felt where she'd touched. "It's sore, all right," he said. "My mother's going to think I've been in the wars when she sees me." How strange. He hadn't even known that one of Frank Flynn's punches had landed. At least this one wouldn't need stitches.

"Good-night, then, old chap," Mr. Bensonhurst said. The words sounded so English and so wrong in that American accent that Barry had to smile.

"Good-night."

"I wanted you to know," Mrs. Adair said softly. "I didn't like it that you thought me a monster."

"I never thought that," Barry said. He watched them go together down the wide staircase, and he was glad for them and glad for Jocelyn. It might be a long way to go, but in the end they'd be a family. Wasn't that something his own mother had said, too?

He turned and looked again at the

< 152 >

swinging doors to the deck. The thought that Pegeen might come had crept far into the back of his head. Just because by now she'd have read the letter, what made him think she would come right away up onto the cold deck? Why had he ever thought she would? And how long had he been standing here talking to Mrs. Adair and Mr. Bensonhurst? Five minutes. Maybe ten.

It was what Father Dooley in Mullinmore would have called an act of blind faith, but a fool action for all of that, that made him push open the door and go out again into the cold to wait. *But,* he told himself, *just in case.*

He thought he'd waited a long time, but maybe it only seemed long with the cold sinking through him and his ears nervous at every sound, at every creak and twitch of the ship. Easy to tell himself the fighting Flynns wouldn't be after him tonight, but his muscles didn't seem to believe him. They jerked and tightened and his fingers fumbled around till they found the little knife in his pocket.

He'd never seen stars so hard and

< 153 >

sharp edged. He'd never seen a sea so calm, like a mirror of glass.

Then she was there. She had wrapped herself again in the shawl. It hid her hair and turned her into a shapeless bundle of black. The silver pin at her neck gleamed through the weave of the wool.

"Jonnie brought the life jackets," she said. "Thank you. But I thought maybe there was more you wanted to say to me."

"There is." His mouth was so numbed with cold that the words wouldn't come. He wished she'd worn the long black coat that came almost to her ankles, because the cold was desperate, sinking through flesh and bones, turning the marrow inside them to ice.

"Let's go inside," he muttered.

Pegeen pulled away. "Och, no. What if one of the stewards saw me and sent me back to my rightful place? I'd die of shame."

She would, he knew. But it was so cold.

"We could go down to steerage, then," he said. "We can't be out here— you can't."

"No, Frank and Jonnie might be around."

< 154 >

Well, he didn't want that either. The whistle might not save him next time.

"Just tell me fast what it is you want," Pegeen said.

Everything jumbled in his head. The danger to the ship, if there was danger. That she should be ready if anything happened.

He stared at her, not knowing where to begin or how to make sense. Did she know that he liked her? Which was daft. Did she know?

"It was mostly the life jackets," he said. "I was worried you might need them."

And then there was a sudden gentle jolt, a ripping sound as if someone had drawn a knife along the outside of the ship, the way Jonnie Flynn had drawn his knife across Grandfather's carriage way back in Mullinmore. There was a fumbling sound, like marbles rolling along the deck, thousands and thousands of marbles.

"What . . . ?" Pegeen clutched at his arm. "What was that? Look!" She was pointing over his shoulder. "Look!"

Sailing past them, towering above the deck where they stood, so close that if a

< 155 >

person leaned over the railing a person could touch it, was a ghostly white shape. They stared at it, speechless, as it passed them, or as they passed it.

"Was it another ship?" Pegeen whispered. "One of those old-fashioned ships with great white sails? But sure there aren't any of those anymore, only in paintings. Did it bump into us? I felt a bit of a thump."

"I . . . I . . . ," Barry began. "It was an iceberg. We just missed it. Maybe it touched us."

In the strange white light it seemed as if a thousand stars had fallen from the sky. They lay small and glittering on the deck. Barry fumbled to pick one up. It shone on his glove. "Ice!" he said.

And at that moment he heard far away in the depths of the ship a dull sound that he'd never heard before, but knew. The distant metal thump of a watertight door coming down, and another, and another. *Like traps,* he thought. *Like guillotines falling.*

They stood in terrified silence as the *Titanic* came to a smooth, silent stop.

< 156 >

Barry hadn't much noticed the steady beat of the engines but he noticed the silence when they stopped. The *Titanic* lay motionless. There was no small push of air as the ship glided forward, no whisper of waves against the hull. For a semisecond he imagined the ship hanging between sky and sea, between time and space, suspended in nothingness. The quiet was more eerie than noise could ever be.

Pegeen had her hands pressed against her cheeks. "Why have we stopped?"

"I don't know."

A crush of noise and people erupted

< 157 >

through the doors and onto the deck. Questions were shouted back and forth. Crowds rushed to peer across the ocean, calm and aglimmer under the stars.

Barry and Pegeen ran across to the railings with them. He could hardly believe what they'd seen a few minutes ago. But they couldn't both have imagined it.

Then someone pointed. "My gosh! Look at the iceberg . . . way behind us. Hurry! Quick, it's drifting away."

Barry leaned across the railing as far as he dared. Little lumps of ice shattered under his boots. Floating behind them, blue-white, shining, the iceberg sailed majestically on. It was like a mountain, the kind Barry had seen in postcards of the Alps or the Matterhorn, sheer and sleek.

"Do you think that's why we stopped?" The woman who asked was wearing a Chinese silk dressing gown with a dragon that flamed red and gold from hem to collar. She hugged her arms around herself and the wide, pleated sleeves swept out like fans. "Brrr," she said. "It's so cold. But I had to find out what's going on."

< 158 >

"I felt a bump," someone said.

"Felt a bump? I was in my bunk and the ice came tumbling in through my open porthole," a man in pajamas and a raccoon coat said. "I'll tell you, I've never leapt out of bed faster."

"Look at this, would you?" Someone scooped up one of the ice chips that littered the deck. "Hey, I'd like to take this home for a souvenir. Do you think it will melt?"

"Not if it stays this cold, it won't."

Pegeen stood in front of Barry, not speaking, keeping herself unnoticed. He put his hands on her shoulders, feeling how bony they were, like a bird's wings, so small, so delicate even through the bulkiness of his gloves. He wondered how he could get his gloves off and his hands back on her shoulders without her noticing. He could smell the faint smell of moth balls off her shawl, the kind Grandmother kept in the wardrobes at home.

A steward who came along the deck was instantly surrounded.

"Can you tell us what's wrong?"

"Not a thing, sir. An iceberg came

< 159 >

close, that's all I know. I think we shaved the side of it. Nothing to worry about."

"Someone said he thought he heard the watertight doors close."

"It's possible, madam. If so, it was just a precaution. 'Safety first' is the White Star motto. I'm sure we'll be under way again in a few minutes." His smile showed big, caramel-colored teeth. "Then you'll hear the doors go up. You know what they say, madam. What goes up must come down. And vice-versa."

"Well, I'm going inside. I'm freezing."

"I would certainly recommend that, madam. There's nothing to see anyway."

And there wasn't, anymore. Just the quiet, peaceful, starlit emptiness of the ocean.

An officer came hurrying in the opposite direction, heading for the bridge.

"Do you have any information?" a man asked him, a man fully dressed in a coat with a fur collar, overboots on top of his shoes. Barry saw that he was carrying a life jacket that he kept behind his back as though ashamed to be seen with it.

< 160 >

"We may have dropped a propeller blade. That's the guess down in the officers' room. If that's the case we'll have to return to Belfast for repairs."

"Back to Belfast?" The woman in the Chinese robe was now also wrapped in a blanket that had mysteriously appeared. "What a dreadful bore. Whoever wants to go back to Belfast?"

"Well, I'm going back to my bridge game," another passenger said grumpily. "I hope my partner hasn't given up and gone to bed."

"Hey, come up here and see the snowball fight," someone called from the railing that overlooked the poop deck.

Ice had really broken off the berg onto the lower deck. Great chunks, some soft and powdery as snow, lay scattered there like boulders. A half-dozen third-class passengers were laughing and whooping and throwing ice balls at each other. Barry saw Jonnie Flynn cramming ice down the neck of Mick Kelly's jersey; Mick, all puffed up in his life jacket, screamed and hopped about, trying to fish it out.

"Jonnie'll kill me if he sees me up

< 161 >

here," Pegeen said, and stepped back. "I'd better go."

"I suppose," Barry said. He wondered if he should try warning her again about a coming disaster. Maybe it had to do with this iceberg, though nobody seemed worried.

When he turned around he saw Colonel Sapp behind him. The colonel had a glass in his hand, and he took a sliver of ice off the deck and dropped it into his drink.

"Bit of bad seamanship there, I'd say," he boomed in his parade-ground voice. "Still, not everyone can ice up his drink with ice from an iceberg, what?"

"It will make a good story for your collection," Barry said, and the colonel gave him a suspicious stare. He eyed Pegeen from top to toe.

"I don't believe I've met the lady."

Instantly Barry knew, by the emphasis on the word "lady," that the colonel understood Pegeen was a steerage passenger and was not a person he would ever call a lady in the real sense of the word. How did the colonel fix her place so quickly?

< 162 >

Was it the black shawl, the kind that factory workers and poor country women wore? Was it the way she kept her head lowered, didn't speak? Barry felt anger building inside him. He wanted to kick the colonel's teeth in.

"This is Miss Pegeen Flynn, Colonel Sapp," he said, willing Pegeen to lift her eyes and be the person she'd been down in steerage, sure of herself, proud and confident.

"How do you do, sir," Pegeen said, and bobbed her knee, the servant to the master.

Barry stared. How could she? Bowing like that to silly old Colonel Sapp!

"Huh." The colonel muttered something else unintelligible. "Well, I'm going back inside," he said to Barry. "There's obviously nothing to be seen out here, and it's cold enough to freeze an Eskimo's eyeballs." He lowered his voice. "Mr. and Mrs. Jacob Astor are in the reception room. I had the good fortune to have the table next to them and I caught a word or two of their conversation. Absolutely charming. Lovely people. I hope the

< 163 >

table's still free. Probably not, though. There's always some bounder ready to take advantage." He gave Pegeen a curt nod and turned away.

"Daft old coot," Barry muttered, his anger still hot inside. Before he could stop himself, he added, "You didn't need to lower yourself to him like that. You should have stood up." He'd moved her inside, out of the cold.

"Be quiet, Barry O'Neill," she said, and her voice shook. "Don't you think I'm ready to die of shame at the way I acted? Don't you think I'm wishing I could be different? I'm afraid of the colonels and the captains and the sirs and the ladies. But they've made me be this way. They look down their noses at us. I forgot I'm not still in Ireland and I shouldn't be bowing and scraping to them." She let the shawl fall from around her head and the brightness of her hair made her look pale. "You can be sure I'll learn to be different in America."

"It's just—," Barry began sheepishly, knowing the truth of what she was saying and wishing he'd kept quiet.

< 164 >

"There's no pleasing the likes of you, is there? You want to be bowed to. You don't want us to talk back. If we do we're in trouble, like Frank and Jonnie always are."

Barry swallowed. "I'm sorry, Pegeen—," he began.

"You're not sorry. You don't know anything. You don't know how they treat the Flynns in Mullinmore."

"We never treated you badly." It was Barry's turn to be angry. "My grandpop wouldn't. My grandmother wouldn't."

"They don't treat us any way. They don't see us, but them that works for them does. That Bowers, and that Dickie that drives for your grandparents." She spit out the word "Dickie" as if it tasted sour in her mouth.

"Bowers and Dickie?" Barry wanted to reach out, touch her cheek, tell her again he was sorry, but it would be no use. They were standing at the top of the grand staircase. From the smoking room came the sound of men's voices raised in laughing argument.

"I was hoping you could take the first

< 165 >

five tricks," someone said loudly. There was a gust of laughter.

"Keep dreaming," someone else said. The mighty bridge game going on. Bridge as usual.

A smoking-room steward passed, balancing a small silver tray with four glasses on it. "Excuse me, sir, madam," he said politely to Pegeen and Barry.

Everything was the same, except that the great glass dome over their heads was perfectly still, not rattling its sweet, silvery rattle in accompaniment to the ship's movement. Everything was the same, except that the engines had stopped and a great mountain of ice had just passed them by.

"I'll walk you to your cabin, Pegeen," Barry said. "Didn't Mick Kelly say it's all right to walk you to the cabin door and no further? We'll take the elevator down."

"Thanks, but I'll go the way I came, and I'll go by myself." She held out her hand. "I'll say good-bye. I'm not thinking we'll see each other again till we land, and probably not then." This time he took off his glove. Her hand was ice-cold and so

< 166 >

were the eyes that looked directly into his. If there had once been stars in them for him, they weren't there now.

"Good-bye." He watched her push open the doors to the deck. "Can't I at least walk you back?"

"No," she said without looking at him, letting the doors slam flat behind her.

It took him a minute standing there to get himself together. Hard to believe he felt so lost and alone. He didn't know Pegeen Flynn. She was nothing to him. But if they *had* dropped a propeller blade, and if they *did* have to go back to Belfast, wouldn't he see her then? There'd be time. They could get to know each other. While they waited for the ship to be fixed, the White Star Line would probably put the passengers in a hotel, the Grand Central or the Wellington.

Not the third-class passengers, though. The White Star Line would find them decent digs somewhere like the Shore Road or Grosvenor Street.

Barry hit his hand against the side of his head, forgetting the bruise that Mrs. Adair had warned him about, feeling it

< *167* >

start to jump and throb. He was thinking that way again. First class here, third class there. "They've made me be this way," Pegeen had said. Well, they'd made him this way, too, or he'd made himself. "It'll be different in America," she'd said. That would be good.

He went slowly down the stairs, past the Café Parisien. Inside he could see people seated at the little wicker tables. The ship's orchestra was playing at the far end of the café, almost hidden by the potted plants. Two couples were dancing. He didn't see Mrs. Adair; probably she'd gone below in case the bump had wakened Jocelyn and frightened her.

When he got to his own cabin he saw that Mr. Scollins was awake and reading in bed. He had his gems and jewels book open across his chest.

"What a botheration," he said to Barry. "Nothing ever works right anymore. Our Mr. Billings got one of those new cash registers for the shop—we couldn't get it to open properly. They had to send one of their men three times before we got it right. But who would think a ship like the *Titanic* would have a prob-

< 168 >

lem? Someone's head is going to roll for this."

"Have you seen Watley?" Barry asked.

"He went to find out how long we will be delayed. I do think someone might make an announcement, at least to the first-class passengers. I'm anxious in case my New York firm will blame me if I don't turn up on schedule."

"You can send them a wireless tomorrow," Barry said, only half listening. He took off his gloves and cap and scarf and tossed them on the bed. The whistle gleamed silver in the cabin light, and he slid it inside against his skin. Pegeen was probably right about how the poor were treated in Ireland. But given half a chance, the Irish poor would treat the rest of them pretty badly, too. If he hadn't had his whistle tonight, they'd have murdered him dead, wouldn't they? He went to the mirror to take a look at his face.

There was a discreet knock and Watley came in. He stood just inside the door, his hands folded in front of him.

"Mr. O'Neill, Mr. Scollins, I'm afraid I have some disturbing news."

Scollins groaned. "I knew it. We're

< 169 >

going to be delayed for hours and hours."

"I have been below," Watley said. "The sea has broken through to Boiler Room Five and Boiler Room Six. I'm afraid the iceberg came rather too close and sliced the side of the ship. The water-tight doors are closed fast, and I'm told there is no danger. The *Titanic,* as you know, is unsinkable." He looked straight at Barry, his dark, hooded eyes expressionless. "But I must advise you and my other passengers to dress warmly and put on your life jackets. I will guide you to your lifeboat stations."

"We're to go outside? On deck? Now, in the middle of the night?" Scollins was getting more and more irritated with every question. He swung his legs out of the bed. "Is this an emergency practice, or something equally ridiculous? I'd say stopping the ship and giving us alarming messages is going too far."

"It is not a drill, Mr. Scollins. I beg you to take this seriously and do as I say. Do you require assistance with your life jackets, or may I leave you and attend to my other passengers?"

< *170* >

"We can manage," Barry said. He paused. "Watley, can the ship stay afloat if two of the watertight compartments fill up?"

"They say it will stay afloat even if six are flooded," Watley said.

"And," Scollins urged, "if the watertight doors are down the water can go no farther?"

Watley bobbed his head. "That is the theory, sir. I will be back shortly."

Scollins and Barry stood in silence while Watley left on his quiet little feet.

Then Scollins sat heavily on the edge of his bed. "I just don't believe it," he said. "I don't believe it."

Barry stood, trying to imagine Boiler Rooms 5 and 6, the green sea roaring around pipes and valves. Steam hissing. Had any of the boilermen been trapped when those doors slammed down?

In a vague way he noticed that the bed curtains on Scollins's bed hung at a slight angle instead of straight. He blinked and looked again. They were definitely off center, like a picture a little bit crooked on a wall. The door of his own wardrobe

< 171 >

swung open and stayed that way. He walked across. His clothes hung at a slight angle, too, and when he latched the door it swung open again, as if the ship itself were not quite straight, as if it had dipped a little at the bow. *Water weight,* he thought. *Boiler Rooms 5 and 6, and the sea heavy inside them.*

< 172 >

Watley led a mixed group of eight up to the boat deck. Barry was the youngest. There was one very old lady whose name was Mrs. Welsh. She walked with a cane and she had to be helped by a younger one who wore a white uniform under her long traveling coat. Mrs. Welsh had trouble with the stairs, which Watley said they should use instead of the elevators. Barry worried about Pegeen. Was she being helped up out of third class by Miss Acheson? At least she had her life jacket with her now.

A man racing down the stairs yelled to them as he passed, "They're going to put

< 173 >

us in lifeboats and take us out. I'm off to get an extra blanket. What a caper! No one's going to believe us when we get back home."

"A ride in a lifeboat?" Mrs. Welsh exclaimed. "I'm certainly not going for a ride in any lifeboat."

"There, there." The nurse kept pushing Mrs. Welsh's life jacket away from her chin so it would be more comfortable.

Barry moved next to Watley and whispered so no one else could hear, "Aren't you going to tell them it's not a caper, that there could be real danger?"

"That is not my job, Mr. O'Neill. It's the captain's," Watley whispered back. "I would be exceeding my authority. The captain has his own faith in the *Titanic*. He will not want to alarm the passengers."

Alarm, Barry thought. *Terrify might be more like it.*

Among their group was a priest, the bottom half of a silver cross dangling below his life jacket; Mrs. Welsh; her nurse; an older man in a tweed overcoat and Sherlock Holmes cap; and two women who seemed to be sisters, very sedate and

< 174 >

solemn. He and Mr. Scollins made up the eight. None of them seemed as alarmed as he was. None were terrified.

"You told me," Barry said. "Why won't you tell them?"

Watley didn't turn his head. "Perhaps telling you was a mistake," he said. "It was an unfortunate impulse brought on by our prior conversations."

"Well, tell me something else." It was hard to talk without being overheard, and Barry knew being overheard would make the mistake worse. People could panic, and maybe for no reason. "Is this the disaster you warned me about?"

"Why are you whispering?" Mrs. Welsh asked irritably. "I won't be kept uninformed. Just because I am old doesn't mean I have lost my wits."

"No indeed, madam," Watley said smoothly. "I consider you to be a lady of great intelligence."

"Yes," Mrs. Welsh said. "Now, let's get on with this nonsense."

The boat deck outside was crowded, but it felt like a party arranged on a too-cold night. Passengers stood in clumps to

< 175 >

keep warm; stomped their feet, blew on their fingers. Breath froze in the air.

The man on the stairs had been right, though; they *were* doing something with the lifeboats. Barry watched the little cluster of seamen swarming over the lifeboats that were there, taking off the canvas covers. Others were passing lanterns and tins of food to be stored on the boats.

In his mind Barry heard Howard's voice again, "Not enough lifeboats. Not enough."

Mr. Scollins looked dazed. He had dressed himself completely in a dark suit and waistcoat, the hard-collared shirt and striped tie he'd worn to board the *Titanic* at Queenstown. He could have been going to a jewelers' convention, except for the life jacket strapped on top. Even the watch chain was looped across his chest, and he kept pulling the watch from his pocket to look at it, fumbling it back under the life-belt straps. His face had the same greenish tinge it had had when he was seasick.

Barry wondered if he were green himself. He felt green. His mind churned and foamed, and his stomach with it. He

< 176 >

wished he didn't know about those flooded boiler rooms. Better to be at a boat party than standing here shivering, frightened, and unsure.

Now the crew was fitting cranks into the davits and uncoiling the lines. The cranks turned, the pulleys squealed, and one of the boats swung out from the ship to hang level with the deck.

He had to find Pegeen. Hurriedly he pushed his way through the crowd, ignoring Watley's shout of "Mr. O'Neill!" He edged around talking, laughing groups.

"Think of the stories," someone was saying. "We'll probably get headlines in the *Times* — '*Titanic* Passengers Brave Cold on Deck for Safety Drill.' "

Lady, lady, Barry thought. He had the urge to wave his arms, to shout and scream, "You idiots. Take this seriously. Have you thought this might not be a drill? Have you thought it might not be a joke?"

Up toward the bow he thought he saw Pegeen, and he half ran, thinking how he'd tell her, what he'd say to her. He'd stay with her. Bring her back with him.

But it wasn't Pegeen. There was no

< 177 >

sign of her or of Mary or Mick Kelly, or of Jonnie or Frank Flynn either. None of them. He stopped an officer rushing by. "The third-class passengers. Where would they be?"

The officer shrugged off his hand. He had a sheaf of papers and was obviously in a hurry.

"I have no idea. They're probably being kept on another deck."

Barry held on to his sleeve, striding fast beside him to keep up. "Another deck— C, maybe?"

"Naturally the captain doesn't want all the passengers on the same deck. Do you know how many passengers there are on this ship? They'll be brought up when it's time," the officer said.

C. Two decks down.

Barry raced down the grand staircase. Were the stairs at a slope, too? No, he was imagining it. Still, he held on to the banister.

He went quickly around C Deck, looking at everyone. There were people standing about in groups, some sitting on the long wooden chairs. Nobody that he

< 178 >

knew, nobody. Where were the third-class passengers? He went back again to the boat deck.

"I told you this ship was doomed," a doom-filled voice behind Barry said. It was Howard, with his wife, Mrs. Cherry Hat, standing just inside the doors to the boat deck.

"Oh, this is just a simulation, old chap," a hearty man said, pushing to get out himself. "Get in the spirit of the thing. I intend to be on the first lifeboat away, just as I'd be if it were a real shipwreck."

"It is a real shipwreck, and you won't be on the first boat away," Howard said; but he sounded sad, not irritated. "How old are you, son?" he asked Barry.

"Fifteen, sir."

Howard shook his head, and Barry's heart gave another sickening lurch. What did Howard mean by that mournful shake of his head?

Mrs. Cherry Hat was wearing lipstick that had probably been a cheeky red when she put it on, but it looked purple out in the deck lights. She hadn't done a very good job of it. Her lips looked lopsided,

< 179 >

like the curtains on the bed, Barry thought. Like his clothes in the wardrobe. Like that chandelier. Everything sliding down toward the bow . . . He shifted his glance to the deck, looking for a slant forward, but there was nothing to see except the smooth wooden planks, so beautifully made and level as a tabletop. Nothing but the shoes and boots of the people milling around, the trailing hems of coats, a couple of grips set close to their owners' feet. Up here everything seemed normal.

Howard took his wife's arm. "I think we'll go 'round to port side," he told Barry. "I'd like to know what's going on over there. If it's any better." Suddenly and unexpectedly he grasped Barry's hand and shook it. "Good luck to you, young man. Remember, if the ship goes down and you are on it, swim for dear life, get away. There will be a lot of suction when it goes, and it will take you with it. That's how a lot of lives were lost on the *Titan*."

His wife gave a little sob and hid her face on his shoulder. "It's so cold," she whispered. "The sea's so cold. I don't want to die. I don't want to die."

< *180* >

Barry felt her terror rising in a cloud around him. She hung limp and boneless as an empty coat on Howard's arm. "Don't leave me, Howard. Don't leave me. Don't . . ." Her words were a dirge said over and over, running together till they made no sense. Barry could still hear her as she and Howard disappeared among the crowds on the deck.

Around Barry, others were laughing and calling out cheery invitations. "See you in the smoking room when we get the drill over. A nightcap sounds good right now."

"It isn't for real, is it?" a woman asked nervously, hunching her shoulders against the cold.

"Of course not," another reassured her. "There would have been a warning siren if it were real. There has to be. I'm sure that's the law."

There'd been nothing. Barry forced himself to take a deep breath. The cold air seared his lungs. He knew it took three breaths to calm a person down, but tonight one would have to be enough.

< 181 >

Watley moved his group back against the bulkhead. "We will wait here for further instructions," he said. He had his life jacket on like the rest of them, and for the first time Barry noticed that he was carrying the green-patterned box. Inside would be the caul, cobweb fine, gray as old goose grease.

When Barry looked up he saw that Watley was watching him, not speaking. *A penny in his slot*, Barry thought. *A penny in his slot and he'll spit out a card and I'll know what's going to happen next.*

He jumped at the sound of Scollins's voice. "Mr. Watley," Scollins said, "if we do have to go in one of those boats I must have my bag with me, the one I left with the purser for safekeeping. I gave my word to Mr. Billings and Mr. Fetters. You will watch out for Mr. O'Neill?"

"You may trust me," Watley said. "But if you must go, please go quickly. The purser will be busy taking care of passengers' requests for their valuables."

Scollins nodded. "I understand. I will not delay."

Barry watched him go. He was still thinking about those third-class passen-

< 182 >

gers. Where were they? Why, they were on the poop deck, of course. Their own deck. That's where the crew would be holding them until it was time to come up.

He waited till he saw Watley in conversation with another steward, then edged away, back to the promenade deck, where he could look over the railing. This was where he'd stood to watch the dancing, where he'd lost his glove, where he'd seen Pegeen dancing with her skirt ballooning out around her. Looking down now, he saw two couples on the deck, standing there staring across the ocean. No one else. No Pegeen.

Up the stairs again, yet another time. Back to where Watley and the others stood.

The Goldsteins and her brother, Arthur, had stopped next to their little group.

"Do you know, it is our anniversary today," Mrs. Goldstein told Barry. "It's after midnight now, so it's April fifteenth." She was wearing the leather flying cap with the ear flaps, but her face looked smaller somehow and had lost its healthy glow.

< 183 >

"This trip was our treat to ourselves." Mr. Goldstein pulled one of the leather ear flaps and smiled lovingly down at his wife.

Barry had seen Bowers pull one of the hound's ears like that, softly, gently. But he hadn't been that soft and loving to the Flynns back in Mullinmore. Hadn't Pegeen said so?

"I have arranged for the orchestra to play your favorite song tonight, my dear," Mr. Goldstein added.

Mrs. Goldstein smiled wanly. "I'll like that." Did they really believe there would be a tonight? Barry wondered. Or did they suspect, and were they putting on an act for each other and for him?

"What is your favorite song?" he asked.

" 'Come Where My Love Lies Dreaming,' " Mr. Goldstein said. "And . . ." He paused dramatically. "Arthur here has ordered a cake for us, too."

"We'd be pleased if you'd come over to our table after dinner and share in our festivities," Arthur said.

"Thank you," Barry told him.

< *184* >

"Look behind you. Now what are they up to?" Arthur asked.

Barry saw that some of the boats were being lowered even further so they'd hang alongside Promenade Deck A directly below.

"They'll probably have some of us go down there," Mr. Goldstein said. "There'll be less confusion when we have to get in."

"You think they're really going to put us into the boats?" his wife asked.

Mr. Goldstein shrugged. "It seems that way."

Barry turned to look across the pale, calm ocean that surrounded them, and there was only quiet and beauty. How could anyone believe that there was danger out there?

"Will the women and children kindly go down the stairs to Promenade Deck A," a loudspeaker boomed. "Women and children only."

"Why don't you go down?" Mr. Goldstein said to his wife.

"Without you? Certainly not," Mrs. Goldstein said. She paused. "Perhaps,

< 185 >

though, you should go, Barry. How old are you?"

It was the second time tonight he had been asked that question.

"Fifteen," he said.

There was a silence. "You know," Mrs. Goldstein said, "if you're asked your age by a crew member it might be wise to take off a year or so."

"He wouldn't want to do that, my dear," Mr. Goldstein said gently. "He wouldn't want to be less than honorable."

Barry felt that chill again. That horrible, sickening chill, colder than the air around him, colder than the sea ice.

"But he's only a boy, Samuel," Mrs. Goldstein whispered. "He's only a child."

"Nevertheless, my dear. There will be younger children."

Barry's eyes met Mr. Goldstein's. They knew. This wasn't a drill, and the Goldsteins knew it, too.

Mrs. Welsh, who was being urged toward the stairs by Watley and her nurse, was protesting in a bad-tempered voice. "Go down the stairs now? I just came up the stairs. And are you proposing I get

< 186 >

into one of those . . . ?" She pointed with her cane. "I'm much too old for night cavortings. I shall stay where I am."

Would Grandmother have gone? Probably not, Barry decided. And certainly not without Grandpop.

"There's plenty of time, Mrs. Welsh," the nurse said soothingly. "And plenty of lifeboats. You don't need to make the decision right away. Isn't that so, Mr. Watley?"

"I shouldn't wait," Watley said.

"I intend to wait." Mrs. Welsh gave the deck a thump with her cane.

"Do as you please, madam."

Watley was urging the two solid, sedate women toward the stairs, counting the rest of them. "One, two, three . . ."

Like a tour guide, Barry thought. *Like the men and women who show people around Saint Patrick's Cathedral, the guide standing very still, counting. Waiting to make a speech about the beauty of the stained-glass windows or the wood carvings in the sanctuary.* He felt a terrible longing to be there, smelling the mustiness of the carpet, the hot wax of the candles

< 187 >

flickering against the altar. So familiar. So much a part of home. So safe.

Women and children were trooping past them toward the stairs. Small children, Barry noticed, either up in their mothers' arms or straddling the humps of the life jackets or holding their mothers' hands.

His mother would be looking forward to him coming. What if he never came? What if they never got to know each other? She'd cry. He remembered her crying the last time she and his father had left him. This would be worse, though. He felt the burn of tears in his own eyes.

The ship's band suddenly appeared on deck, all eight of them. Bandmaster Hartley and his men had been playing in the first-class lounge. Now they had moved to the boat deck, near the entrance to the grand staircase. Their music added to the party air. Did they know about the flooded compartments as they played "The Tales of Hoffman"? Grandmother could play that, too, on the piano.

The small group of women and children who had gone down the stairs came tromping back up. One of them, not

< 188 >

much older than Barry, looked at him and giggled. "They haven't an idea what they're doing around here," she said. "They forgot there are glass windows on the promenade deck. Nobody knew how to get them open, and there we were, the boats on the outside and us on the inside. Mama says the crew on this ship couldn't organize a Sunday-school picnic."

"At least we got our exercise for this evening," someone said, and Mrs. Welsh boomed in a loud, triumphant voice, "Didn't I tell you it would be better to stay where you are?"

One of the officers waved the group over to where he stood by one of the upper lifeboats. Barry remembered him from the bridge. His name was Murdoch. "Come over here, please," he called. "I'm asking only for women and children."

Nobody moved. "This is so silly," someone complained. "Honestly."

"Come on, come on!" Murdoch shouted.

One woman stepped nervously forward. "Are you sure we have to?"

"Mind your step." Murdoch held out his hand to help her in.

< 189 >

"Do you have your pass with you to get back on board, Elizabeth?" a woman called from somewhere back in the crowd. "You can't get back on the *Titanic* without a pass, you know, and it'll be a long row home."

"So amusing," someone said.

"Six cents a ride. Once around the big boat and back," a man bellowed, and there were gales of laughter.

Why wasn't anybody taking this seriously? Barry wondered. Because it seemed impossible. Unthinkable. Unsinkable.

Another woman with two little children and a baby was next to get in the lifeboat.

"Wave good-bye to Papa," she told them, and they waved and blew kisses. "We'll be back soon."

Barry wondered about Mrs. Adair and Jocelyn and Malcolm. They were probably over on the port side. The third-class passengers might be there, too. Pegeen, her black shawl clutched around her. Pegeen with her friends and no thought of him. No real understanding of the danger.

Several more women had scrambled on board the lifeboat. Two seamen were

< 190 >

already in charge, one at the rudder, the other helping with the boarding. Still the lifeboat was almost empty.

"We need some more ladies," Officer Murdoch yelled.

"No chance," someone called. "I'm staying here. I'm not going to swing down in that little thing and maybe have it tip and throw us all into the sea."

"I didn't think of that." The mother who'd boarded with her two children and baby stood again, ready to get out.

"You'll be all right, missus. We'll get you there safely," the sailor at the tiller said. "Just sit back down."

They sat shivering, huddled on the hard wooden benches, their faces shriveled with cold.

"Come on, I need more women and children." Murdoch was getting impatient and angry.

A man stepped forward. A pale, thin gentleman, moving furtively as if he were ashamed.

"I asked for women and children," Murdoch said too loudly, and the pale man shrunk back.

"Jolly bad form, that," someone close

< 191 >

to Barry muttered. "The fellow's not a gentleman."

"I'll go if my husband can go with me," a woman called out. She and her husband wore matching checked motor coats under their life jackets, and they stood close together, holding hands.

"Oh, all right." Murdoch's voice was sharp with exasperation. "I'll take some couples, but only couples. We can't wait much longer."

The thin man edged forward.

"Married couples only," Murdoch said, and he waved to the man the women and children had called good-bye to. "You, please get aboard."

Barry elbowed Mrs. Goldstein. "You and Mr. Goldstein could go now. You're a couple."

"And leave Arthur?" Mrs. Goldstein asked.

"Of course, leave me," Arthur said. "I'll be perfectly fine."

"We came together and we'll stay together," Mrs. Goldstein said. Barry thought there were tears in her eyes. "You are my dear brother," she said, "and I am not leaving you."

< 192 >

She gave Barry a push. "Go, Barry. They'll let you on now. They may not later. Say you're thirteen—say you're only thirteen."

Barry took a step forward, then stopped. There'd be safety of sorts in that little boat, but he'd look like a terrible fool, or a coward, or both, like the pale, thin man who was not a gentleman. And the lifeboat did seem so frail and small hanging there. He stole a glance along the sturdy, substantial deck of the *Titanic*. With two compartments flooded it would still float. Watley had said that. Everybody knew it. The ship could probably float forever. Besides, he wasn't going anywhere till he found Pegeen.

"Mr. Scollins would have a fit if I left without him," he said, "and I'm not a couple."

"Lower away," Mr. Murdoch called, and the first lifeboat began its slow creak downward. Barry counted seventeen in the boat, which was supposed to hold fifty-four. He moved back beside Watley.

"Why doesn't he fill it up?" Barry asked.

< *193* >

"He's in a hurry," Watley said, "and the women don't want to go. Not yet, they don't," he added, his fingers stroking the top of the green-patterned box.

The *Titanic* railings were crowded as the passengers watched the first lifeboat go, crank by crank, toward the ocean far below.

"It's like the swing boats at the fair, Dorothy," a young woman said.

"I know. Remember how dizzy I was when we went on one of those things? I was dizzy for days."

Peering down like this, Barry could see that the ocean was awash with ice that floated in flat, pale chunks like surface ice sloshing on a lake. No bergs, though. No great white mountains to bear down on the little boat and crush it beneath tons of ice.

There was a cheer when the lifeboat settled with a splash on the surface, wobbled, and righted itself. From up here the sea looked calm, but there must be a roll to it. The lifeboat tossed around.

"Oh, look at it jiggle," somebody said. "I'd be sick as a blooming dog."

< 194 >

The small figures in their white blurs of life jackets waved up at them.

"I bet they're freezing. Where are the gangplanks? They'll need to put gangplanks down for them to get back on board."

"Ahoy there!" someone shouted through cupped hands, but a sudden whoosh and a hiss took their attention from the boat below to the sky above. A burst of blue stars spangled across the sky.

"Fireworks." It was a small boy's voice, high with excitement.

"Twelve forty-five A.M." Watley said, flat and expressionless. "Twelve forty-five A.M. The first boat's away and the RMS *Titanic* has just fired her first distress rocket. We can now pray that there's another ship around to see it."

< 195 >

The first boat down on the starboard side was Number 7. Then Number 5, and it was half-empty, too. Distress flares exploded and died in the sky above them but there was still no rush to the boats. The *Titanic* felt solid as a rock and just as steady. What could be wrong with it? Why would anybody want to exchange it for a little husk of a thing way down there in the big, mysterious ocean?

Mrs. Welsh and her nurse stood close together. Every now and then the older woman would snort and say, "Preposterous. Someone's going to hear about this."

Watley had stopped a deck steward he

< 196 >

seemed to know and had a conversation with him out of the group's hearing. Afterward he glided across to them. "Madam," he told Mrs. Welsh, "I have just been informed that the sea is knee-deep down in H Deck. Our wireless operator is sending out SOS signals. That means we're sinking, madam." Watley spoke in a monotone, with no emotion in his voice or on his face.

The nurse hid her face in her hands. "It's not possible," she whispered.

"It is not only possible, it is a fact." Watley made his little heels-together, head-bobbing bow. "May I escort you to the lifeboat?"

Mrs. Welsh poked him with the point of her stick. "This is the truth, Mr. Watley?"

"I assure you. But there is also good news. The *Carpathia*, another large vessel, is only fifty-eight miles away, and coming fast."

"There!" Mrs. Welsh beamed her triumph. "Nurse and I will simply wait for it to arrive. That will be much more comfortable."

< 197 >

"There will not be time to wait, madam. The *Titanic* has now no more than an hour to live. The words come from Mr. Andrews, the builder of the ship, who is on board and who has checked the damage."

In the stunned silence another rocket whistled into the sky and burst in a hundred pinpoints of light. For a few seconds the four proud funnels were etched against the horizon. The flare lighted the faces upturned to watch it, hundreds and hundreds and hundreds of faces.

A baby was crying.

A little boy ran a toy horse on wheels out along the top of the ship's railing. "Giddyup, giddyup! Go, horsie. Good boy."

And then there was the most world-shattering noise. The *Titanic* was letting off steam through her funnels. It sounded like a great herd of elephants trumpeting their rage. The roar filled the night, bounced off the water, raced to the far edge of the ocean world, then started again. It was never going to stop.

In a terrified rush of imagination Barry

< 198 >

saw the *Titanic* the way the stars would see it. The way God would see it. Lying there big and black and helpless. A great sea creature, bellowing its death cries.

Mouths around him moved, saying soundless words, screaming soundless screams. The mouths seemed impossibly big, impossibly ugly.

Mrs. Welsh motioned with her arm, and she and her nurse moved as quickly as they could, pushing through to the lifeboat that was half-loaded. Mrs. Welsh shook her cane at the officer in charge, and he gave his directions with his hands, calling the old woman and the nurse forward, physically separating husbands from wives, mouthing the words "women and children, women and children" over and over. There was a frantic urgency now. It was as if the braying of the beast had at last opened the gates of panic.

Barry stood on an opened wooden deck chair and peered up and down the slanted deck. Still no Pegeen. He cupped his hands and shouted into the noise, "Pegeen, Pegeen Flynn!" He fumbled to get out his whistle, blasted it full force.

< *199* >

Not a single head turned. The priest who stood next to him had the silver crucifix in his hands. His hands were closed and he was muttering words that Barry couldn't hear over the roaring steam and the chaos all around him.

The prayer, if it was a prayer, made the man in the Sherlock Holmes cap angry. He shouted something and grabbed for the crucifix, but the chain was strong and the priest's grip tight. With a disgusted glance Sherlock turned and vanished into the crowd.

Watley put his hands on Barry's shoulders and propelled him forward. "Go!" he shouted in his ear, and Barry, frightened again beyond thoughts of Pegeen, beyond thoughts of humiliation or honor, went, pushing himself to the front of the group. One hour to live. One hour to live. "Me, me," he shouted along with everyone else.

But Mr. Murdoch waved him back. There was another seaman standing at the side in the shadow of a stanchion. The gun in his hand was half-hidden in the padding of the life jacket.

"Women and children," Officer Mur-

< 200 >

doch mouthed. Easy to read his lips as he repeated the words over and over, like a prayer.

Number 3 was cranking out and down now, filled almost to overflowing.

Barry moved back, ashamed but calmer. He wasn't going to be on any of the boats. He accepted that. Acceptance made it easier. He would have to save himself. But he would. He was young, he was strong, he was a good swimmer. He wasn't going to die. He'd find Pegeen and he'd save her, too.

The roar of the steam stopped, and all other sound with it. The passengers seemed to hold their breath, waiting for what would happen next.

But nothing happened. Nothing different. Little by little, terrified conversations began. "The lifeboats, the lifeboats. Where's Alice? Put her on your shoulders." There was a pell-mell rush to where Murdoch was loading again.

"They're sending Morse light signals from the bridge in all directions," a man shouted. "Nobody's answering them."

"An officer told us there's another ship

< 201 >

stopped in the ice. Where is it? Why aren't they signaling back? Why don't they come through the ice and get us?" The voices were on the edge of panic, shrill and hysterical.

Now Barry could plainly see the slope of the deck. The bow was dipping, the way it would in a small boat going through a storm at sea. Noticeable now. Too easy to see and understand.

Mr. Ryerson stood with his hands on his wife's padded, life-jacketed shoulders. "You must obey orders, my dear," he said calmly. "When they say 'Women and children to the boats,' you must go."

"No, no," she said, and stamped her foot. "No."

The captain had appeared on the boat deck with a loudspeaker. Barry saw an elderly man and woman go up to him.

"Please, Captain Smith," the woman begged. Tears had frozen glistening snail tracks on her face. "Please, can my husband come in a boat with me? I'll be all alone in the world if I lose him."

Captain Smith didn't seem to hear— but Barry could hear every word.

< *202* >

And still he hadn't seen Pegeen. He ran around to the port side.

And there was Colonel Sapp standing against the bulkhead. He was wearing a full-dress army uniform. The medals pinned on his tunic shone through his open greatcoat. He had no life jacket. The deck lights reflected on the shiny peak of his officer's cap, on the gleam of his officer's shoes.

"Colonel Sapp," Barry said.

"Mr. O'Neill." His mustache had been freshly waxed. His eyes were steady. "I have written a letter to my sister in Long Island. Her name is Mrs. John Windermere, like *Lady Windermere's Fan*. You remember it. I gave the letter to a seaman on the Number Eight lifeboat. He promised me if he made it to safety he'd mail it. If you make it, will you telephone her? Tell her I went like an English gentleman and a Guards officer."

"But, Colonel, aren't you going to try?"

"No use to fight the ocean, lad. I'd just as soon do this thing gracefully."

Barry nodded. There was such a

< 203 >

dignity about the colonel. Barry felt humbled and sad. The colonel was a brave man. All those stories Barry had laughed at . . . He held out his hand, wishing he could hug him, cry against those proud khaki shoulders, but the colonel was still the colonel.

"Good-bye," Barry said.

"Good-bye, son."

He had to find Pegeen. How much of the hour was used up now? How much? Twenty minutes? He couldn't think.

He shoved his way through the crowds clambering toward the port-side lifeboats, searching for the red hair, the long black shawl. Searching for any steerage passengers he could recognize. He saw none of them.

A man and a woman leaned across the railing. The woman's hair hung in straggles under the jaunty hat with the glowing red cherries around the brim. Howard and his wife. No time to talk to them, though. No time. He had to find Pegeen.

And then as he hurried behind them he heard the woman singing. Heard the man say, "Sh, my darling, sh," in the most tired, the most hopeless voice Barry had

< 204 >

ever heard. He slowed, stopped, wondering if he should speak to them or not. That singing, though—that awful singing, high and mad, like a drunk on a street corner . . .

Mrs. Cherry Hat turned slowly, as if sensing Barry's terrified gaze—but the look she gave him had no recognition in it. There was no wave. He saw the dash of her purple lipstick, the two spots of red on her thin cheekbones, before she turned back and began the mindless singing again.

Barry edged away, his heart thumping. Poor Mrs. Cherry Hat, and her so filled, before, with life and happiness.

When he glanced fearfully back beyond the railing to the sea below, he saw it was closer now to the level of the deck. He saw the lifeboats in the ocean. They'd been rowed a good distance from the ship and lay there as if watching, waiting. They'd stay away so the ship wouldn't pull them down in its suction, just the way the swimmers in the water would be pulled down if they stayed too close.

Back to the starboard side, kicking and

< 205 >

shoving his way through the crush, to where Watley stood alone, except for the priest, who was intoning the Lord's Prayer.

"Mr. O'Neill, have you seen Mr. Scollins?" Watley asked.

"No."

"I thought he'd be back by now. I think I should go search for him," Watley said. "Stay here, Mr. O'Neill."

Barry clutched at his arm. "Watley?"

Two people were down on their knees now, praying with the priest.

Barry shouted to make himself heard. "Watley, where are the third-class passengers? You have to tell me."

"I don't know."

"They're not up here anywhere."

"I imagine they have been taken to their own deck."

"But this is the only deck that has lifeboats, and they aren't on the poop deck. I've already looked. And why would they be taken there anyway? There aren't any lifeboats. Isn't that right? Isn't that right, Mr. Watley?"

"That is correct, sir. It is possible the

< 206 >

steerage passengers are being held some-place else until it is their turn."

"What do you mean, until it is their turn? There are only a few boats left."

"I know." There was something deep in Watley's eyes, some awful knowledge that chilled Barry's heart.

"You mean they're keeping them below until—"

"I couldn't say, sir."

"You 'couldn't say, sir'?" Barry's rage was choking him. "Damned first-class steward! Damn you, you snob. Just like Bowers and Dickie. Just like all of us. You look out for the Mrs. Welshes, for the me's." In a blur of anger he snatched at the green box, got a hold on the side of it, and pulled it from Watley's hands. The top came off. The caul, shimmering dark under the lights, dropped to the deck between them. Barry stepped back. *I should kick it,* he thought. *I should kick it over to the side and overboard, let it drown with everybody else.* But his foot wouldn't move. His nose dripped, and his eyes, too. He wiped them on the back of Grandpop's glove.

< 207 >

"I'm going," he said.

Watley bent and picked up the caul, and Barry held out the box.

"Thank you." The steward arranged the caul carefully inside, put the lid on.

"I'm going," Barry said again, and Watley bobbed his little bow.

"Come back to this place if you are able, sir. I'll do what I can for you. I won't be saved myself."

Barry stared. "How do you . . . ?"

"I can tell, sir. It is all right. This is how it was meant to be, but not necessarily for you."

"You see that, too?"

"Sometimes I see through a fog, darkly," Watley said. "Do not ask any more. I do not know any more. All our souls are in the hands of the Almighty."

"Right." It was hard getting even that one word out.

Barry let the moving crowd take him then, looking for a door with steps down, so he could find Pegeen. The band was still playing. He knew the tune. Was it a hymn? Was it called "Autumn"? As he pushed his way along the deck, snatches

< 208 >

of music came to him, and with them,
memory—snatches of the words:

> *God of mercy and compassion,*
> *Look with pity on my pain,*
> *Something, something; something,*
> *something,*

and then didn't it say . . .

> *Hold me up in mighty waters,*
> *Keep my eyes on things above.*

Barry shivered.

"All in the hands of the Almighty,"
Watley had said.

Hold us up, he thought. *Oh, please hold*
us up.

< 209 >

CHAPTER 14

An emergency staircase ran from
the boat deck down to E Deck. Barry
had seen it. But where was it? Someone
bumped into him, walking blindly, head
down.

"Watch it—," Barry began. It was Malcolm, Mrs. Adair's friend. They stopped,
facing one another.

"Where are Jocelyn and her mother?"
Barry asked.

"They've gone in one of the lifeboats," Malcolm said. "Pray God they'll
make it."

"But you. Couldn't you?"

"No, and it was touch-and-go at the

< 210 >

end to see if they could both get on. But they did. Charity kept holding up Jocelyn, screaming, 'Take my child! Take my child!' " Malcolm covered his eyes with his hands.

"The boat was that full?" Barry asked.

"Yes. And there were only two boats left. I think. the collapsibles are still here."

Barry gulped down his tears. "It's so unfair. Little Jossie . . ."

"She has her father's handkerchief wadded up in her hand," Malcolm said. "She kept calling for her daddy. I don't know if Jocelyn will ever forgive her mother for taking her from him . . . if they make it. If they're saved."

"I think Jossie will forgive her mother," Barry said. "She'll understand that her mother did everything she could, that she wasn't to blame. My mother—" He stopped. His mother had done all she could, too. The separation wasn't her fault, and now maybe they'd never be together. He bit his lips. "I'm so sorry, Malcolm. You would have made such a wonderful father for Jocelyn. How much

< 211 >

time do you think we have before we sink?"

"I don't know. Someone said a half hour . . . forty-five minutes, not much more. Why don't you stay with me, Barry? We'll try for it together."

"I have to find someone first," Barry said. But was there any use looking? *Save yourself. Save yourself,* something inside him screamed. But he had thirty minutes left. Time to save himself and Pegeen, too.

"Well, cheerio, then." Malcolm smiled a quiet smile.

"Cheerio," Barry repeated.

He ran on, not daring to look back. To have a friend at the end. To be sure of having a friend might make it easier. But if he found Pegeen he'd have her.

Here was a door plainly marked Emergency Stairs.

He yanked it open.

Below him the steps marched down, down, down into the depths of the *Titanic.* Covered lights lit the way, showed Barry the sea below. It was the first time he'd seen it inside the ship, and his heart jumped sickeningly against his ribs. It was

< 212 >

there like water at the bottom of a well, climbing slowly, step by step. Under its pale greenness the lights still gleamed.

"No," he breathed. "No." He'd gone down five, six steps, not really believing what he could see, and he backed up again fast, slamming the door behind him as if slamming it would keep the ocean inside.

Frantically he looked up and down the boat deck, the empty stanchions, all the boats but one gone on this side. The deck was slanting now at a crazy angle, like a seesaw, one end up, the other halfway down. When it dropped all the way, everything would be finished.

There was a sharp scream behind him.

"A woman's fallen. She was trying to jump into one of the boats. But someone caught her ankle—they're pulling her up."

Horror upon horror.

Close to Barry a man had stacked a pile of long wooden deck chairs by the railing and he was heaving them up one by one, then dropping them over. There were two of the round cork life preservers beside him also. RMS *Titanic*. The man paused

< 213 >

for breath. "You never know," he panted. "Throw over anything you see that will float."

Barry nodded. He should help, but more urgent even than that for him was Pegeen. She wasn't anywhere. He ran into the lobby with the grand staircase stretching down. No water coming up these steps yet, but a slope so steep that if he didn't hold on to the banister he'd pitch forward on his face. The cherub clock said 1:20. He had to go almost to the bottom and look back before he could see it. 1:20. How much time left?

A group of about thirty people was coming up the stairs, led by a steward in a white jacket. By their dress and meek manner Barry guessed they were steerage passengers who'd been kept out of the way till the last possible moment. This was the last possible moment. A glance told him Pegeen wasn't among them.

The men and women and children climbed quietly, with no pushing or shoving, trusting sheep following the shepherd. They were used to obeying authority.

< 214 >

"Where are the other third-class passengers?" Barry called to the steward.

He jerked his head. "Below. I'm leading these ones up. They can't find their way in this maze by themselves. I can hardly find it myself. Besides, a lot of the corridors are underwater."

He kept climbing as he talked and Barry had to walk backward in front of him to shout his questions.

"But where are the rest?"

"I doubt if you could find them, and there's not much time. I don't expect there'll be time for me to get back. I was told to bring them up in clusters so there'd be less confusion."

"So what happens to them?"

"They'll be all right, sir."

Barry watched them go, climbing the stairs, quiet and docile. He took a deep, shaky breath. What was the number of Pegeen's cabin? 29G? 27G? But she wouldn't be in her cabin. That whole deck was underwater.

The ocean met him when he dropped down to E Deck, limpid, without a ripple, rising like water in a tub. Dozens of

< 215 >

sodden loaves drifted along what had been the corridor, floating tentacles of raw dough stringing around them. Cabbages, oranges, a straggle of flowers that might once have been a bunch of red carnations. Grandfather always wore a red carnation in his buttonhole to Sunday mass. . . . If he stepped into this water Barry knew he'd be up to his waist. Through the open cabin doors he saw sea lapping over the bottom bunks. Nobody could be here either.

Up again. *Keep going. Don't think of the drowning of Barry Shane O'Neill, his face eaten off by fishes.*

There was another terrible bellow as the *Titanic* blew off more steam. Barry clapped his hands to his ears. He felt as if he were going mad, like Mrs. Cherry Hat. The water had moved up another step. Now it covered his feet, icy cold through his socks and his boots. How much would have to come in before it weighed them down? Was the ship about to turn over, belly-up?

"Help!" he shouted, but his voice was swallowed in the funnel's roar. Or maybe

< 216 >

he'd only screamed the word in his mind.

The roaring stopped and he stood very still, afraid to take another step in case his slightest movement would send the ship spinning to the bottom. Too much silence now. Dead silence.

He would leave here, go up where at least there'd be air.

But what was that other noise? It wafted to him like the murmur of a football crowd in the distance. From where? From his right? Left? The echoes bounced back at him so he couldn't tell.

Down these stairs, along here, ease into a corridor. He stopped when he saw the gates. The closed, locked gates with the seaman on this side of them and the crowd on the other side.

Through the bars he saw Mary Kelly—and Pegeen. His heart soared with joy. Whatever else, he'd found her.

"Pegeen!" he shouted.

And then he was yelling at the seaman. "Hey, you! Why are you keeping them in there? Open that gate and let them out."

The sailor looked startled. "On whose orders? Who are you?"

< 217 >

Was that a shifting of the ship? Had it just lurched and buried itself deeper in the water? There was a silence, as if they'd all felt it. Behind the gates, men and women dropped to their knees, crossed themselves. Barry ran at the man, but the seaman stepped back, his hands in the air. "They can go if they want. I was only doing what I was ordered," he said.

"They told us there was no hurry," someone behind the gate shouted. It was the big-as-a-horse fellow, bigger than ever now in his white life jacket.

"No hurry?" Barry said. No hurry while they all drowned, like kittens locked in a box underwater, clawing to get out.

The seaman was gone, leaving the gate locked behind him.

"We can go?" somebody called. And somebody else said, "Knock the gate down, then." Another voice called, "We shouldn't. We're supposed to stay here till they tell us."

"Don't talk that nonsense anymore, man. We're going."

The crowd ran their shoulders into the

< 218 >

gate again and again till it fell, and they swarmed through.

Why hadn't they done this before, with only a puny gate and one seaman on guard? Barry wondered—and he answered his own question. Because they knew their place. Because he and Grandpop and the rest had taught them they should do only what they were told.

Here was Pegeen. Barry held her hands, the littleness of them smothered in the bigness of his own, bulky in Grandpop's gloves. And then they were running.

"I'm glad I found you," he muttered, not knowing if she heard him or not, but knowing that it didn't matter. He had her.

"Jonnie and Frank and Mick went to find another way," Pegeen said, her voice coming in spurts as they pounded along the corridor through the door, back the way he had come. "How did you get down to us?"

"I don't know for certain," Barry yelled, "and there's no time to talk, Pegeen. Save your breath and run."

But where would they run to? There was no way to tell on this drowning ship,

< 219 >

with nothing level anymore—walls, doors, lights, all hanging at crazy angles. Fire extinguishers rolled under their feet. Broken glass crunched and shattered like ice.

The crowd was separating now, one group going to the left, the other to the right, searching for a way out.

"Keep going against the slant," Barry yelled. "The stern is up. Keep going toward the stern."

"But what can have happened to my brothers?" Pegeen wailed. "They'd have come for us if they'd found a way out. They're trapped somewhere."

"More likely they couldn't find their way back," Barry said. "Keep going, Pegeen. Mary, don't stop for anything."

They rushed this way and that. Barry's wet boots squished with seawater. Were his feet still inside there? Maybe they were black and shriveled, sea-frosted.

Up to the third-class lounge on C Deck. Playing cards scattered, books toppled from shelves, framed pictures of the *Titanic* hanging by one corner. Across the open well deck, holding on to each other to keep from sliding down it. So

< 220 >

cold out here. The sea so close, so icy close. And how strange that it was night and not dark. No moon to light the calm, flat ocean, but the stars so bright it could have been midday.

"Look!" The horse of a fellow was pointing to a thin line of passengers climbing a crane that rose from the after well deck. There was a boom beyond the crane and some of them had reached that, straddling it, edging slowly along with a leg dangling on each side. Where did the boom go? To the railing of the boat deck. A small figure stood up there, waving his arms, urging them on.

"It's my brother Frank!" Pegeen shouted.

From here Barry couldn't tell, but Pegeen could. And then he noticed the red gypsy scarf tied around the person's neck. It *was* Frank!

Barry pushed Pegeen and Mary toward the crane. "Climb," he yelled. There could still be room in those collapsibles. "Climb."

People pressed behind them. "Hurry," they screamed. "Hurry." There was no

< 221 >

holding back now, with the slant of the ship and the sea so close, no way not to be filled with terror. "Hurry!"

"I'll be right after you," Barry whispered to Pegeen. "I'll not let you fall."

Mary went first up the crane, gripping every metal handhold, every span, climbing it like a ladder. Their life jackets made them more awkward than they should have been, but still, black boots found a toehold, numbed hands held tight. Pegeen turned once to look back at Barry and then beyond him to the drop to the deck, or the other way, to the waiting ocean.

"Don't look down," Barry yelled. "Don't look."

They were on the boom now, edging across it, with Frank recognizing them, shouting encouragement. "Come on, Mary girl. Come on, Pegeen. You're doing grand."

Mary was at the railing, Frank helping her across, then Pegeen. Barry.

"You!" Frank began, and Pegeen said, "Are you mad entirely? There's no room for bad feelings on a night like this."

Barry was over, too, onto the deck. He

< 222 >

listened. Could that be the ship's band still playing? It was the hymn he'd heard them playing before. The words churned in his head.

God of mercy and compassion,
Look with pity on my pain.

"Where's Jonnie? Where's Mick?" Pegeen called.

"There's two collapsible lifeboats. They say they're on the roof of the officers' room. One of them's away, but the crew can't get the other one over the side. Jonnie and Mick are trying to help get it free." Frank stopped. "All the real lifeboats are gone, Pegeen. Every one of them. They're gone without us."

Pegeen held her fists against her mouth.

"I know where the officers' quarters are," Barry said before Pegeen and Mary could think more about the other words and what they meant. Pegeen had his hand now and she was holding on to him as if she'd never let go. It was strange how trying to make her feel less terrified helped him to be less terrified himself. . . . "I have

< 223 >

a knife. Maybe I could cut the rope myself on that collapsible."

He stopped. Masses of people were swarming up the boat deck toward them. Hundreds of people. Hordes of people. Screaming, falling, sliding back, clawing for handholds on the slippery, slanted wood. Their shrieks were the shrieks of terrified animals—and then behind them Barry saw that the bow was almost buried in the ocean and that the ship was covered with water halfway along the deck. People flailed about in icy greenness, caught even as they ran, grabbing for each other, for anything that floated, and the sea rushed behind them, swallowing them as it came.

"Get on the railing," he yelled at Pegeen. "Jump!" He fumbled her up. From the railing to the sea was no higher than from the top of a stepladder to the floor.

"Barry, come with me," she screamed. Her shawl had fallen from where she knotted it over her life jacket, and he didn't pick it up. No use. No time. It would drag her down anyway.

Quickly he pulled the whistle on the chain from his neck and put it around

< 224 >

hers. "Hold on to this," he said. "Blow it and I'll come."

Frank was thrusting Mary up. She had one hand on Frank's shoulder and she was screaming, "I can't swim. I can't swim." And Frank said, "The life belt will hold you up, Mary. You have to go." And then Barry saw him slip and go sliding down the deck the way a person would slide down an icy hill on his back, spread out, his hands grasping and finding nothing.

"Frank!" Pegeen was trying to scramble down again herself.

Barry reached up. With one hand he pushed her; with the other he pushed Mary. He heard their flyaway screams, heard the splashes as they hit the water, shouted with all his might. "Swim away from the ship!"

Still holding the railing, he turned. Frank lay spread out on his stomach. People clawed past him and over him, their screams high and piercing as seagulls'.

"Get up, man!" Barry shouted.

"I can't," Frank shouted back.

Barry let himself go, sliding down the deck the way Frank had slid before him.

< 225 >

"My scarf's caught," Frank gasped, one hand going to the back of his neck, the other picking desperately at the knot of the scarf in front. "I can't get it loose here. I can't reach behind myself."

Barry felt underneath Frank's neck. The scarf was hooked on the corner of a ventilator. Frank's weight had pulled it tight.

"Can you get it, man? Can you? It's choking—"

Barry had his glove off, had the little knife out of his pocket, the blade open. A faraway woman's voice inside his head said, "A sweet little souvenir of the *Titanic*. Sweet little souvenir . . ."

Frantically he sawed.

Water lapped around Frank's chest, floated the corner of the gypsy scarf.

The red cotton parted.

Frank slid forward, but Barry had him under the arms, the two of them holding each other, trying to stand.

And then, behind them, Barry heard a different sound. A whooshing as if a great wind were rising—and he looked and saw all the water in the world coming at them.

< 226 >

The wave was big as a house, icy green edged by the yellow deck lights. In it were dark shadows with moving arms and legs, people still struggling as it overtook them. He had one startled glimpse of Mr. Scollins, eyes and mouth agape, the jewel bag in one hand, before the wave caught and devoured him.

Without a second to think, Barry grabbed the strap of Frank's life jacket with one hand, shouted, "Get ready!" and then the wave was on them. The wave took them for itself and carried them with it.

< 227 >

At first he thought he was dead. It was tomb dark and he couldn't breathe. His arms were moving, though, reaching through icy water . . . and then he bobbed up, out into the air, and hung there, gulping and retching. There was noise all around him, screams, howls of agony, pitiful cries as soft as kittens' mewling. Painfully he turned his head and saw other heads in the water around him, hundreds and hundreds of them; saw the dark, floating figures, the blur of the white life jackets; and remembered.

The sinking ship. Frank Flynn. The wave. Feeling was coming back into his

< 228 >

body now. There was pain in every part of him. Frank should be somewhere close. Hadn't they been together? A dark head beside him, a piece of red trapped in the life-belt strap. But why was his face in the water? Why was he looking down through the ocean?

Barry reached out. "Frank!" He caught the hair, turned up the lifeless face, the eyes and mouth open. Frank. He'd drowned, or smashed against something. Barry floated beside him, sick at heart. What could he do? Nothing. Frank was dead.

He must say some words, though, over the dead body, if only because of Pegeen. He touched the back of the wet, lifeless head. "Good-bye, Frank. I tried to be your friend at the end. I hope maybe you had time to know that. God bless. Good-bye." Poor Frank. Poor all of them.

Around him people called names. "John! Helen! Grace!" All around him they called for God—called for help in feeble gasps.

"Pegeen," he screamed. "Where are you?"

< 229 >

He paddled the other way and saw the ship. It was still afloat, its lights glowing eerily both above the water and under it. Only the round stern and the poop deck stuck up out of the ocean, so high, so high up that the small black figures clinging to the railings looked like swarms of bees.

As he watched, the stern rose even higher and the screams grew louder. The first funnel was underwater now. Orange sparks rose from it like embers from a bonfire. In the wash a wooden chair flowed toward him and he grabbed for it, remembering the man throwing the pile of them over, lifetimes and lifetimes ago. The cold was like a thousand knives that cut through him, stuck in his bones. Nobody could live in this cold.

"Pegeen!" he screamed again. And then there was a terrible ripping, tearing noise from the ship, as if her insides were being torn apart, an explosion as the second funnel went under. The lights went out and a great moaning rose from the people in the water. Barry had one last glimpse of the small black bugs on the stern falling, or jumping, in clusters when

< 230 >

the ship stood completely upright as if on her head. Her three giant propellers, like arms, reached for the starlit sky.

Got to get away. Got to get away, there'll be suction. All those people would be pulled down. He would be pulled down. He splashed furiously, getting distance between himself and the ship. When he looked again he saw that the *Titanic* had slipped quietly, soundlessly beneath the ocean. There was nothing to tell where she'd been now, except the dark sea filled with the moving people and the glitter of stars.

Was that a whistle? He stopped his breath. Pegeen! Again.

He tugged the chair with him as he flapped toward the sound, kicking with his numbed legs, the life jacket holding his head out of the water. Once he thought he had her, but it was someone else, someone who clung to him, tried to climb on him, over him, pushing him down. Someone frantic, with claws and staring eyes, whom he had to fight off or he'd be drowned himself.

When he heard the small peep again,

< 231 >

it was almost next to him, and he touched her.

She let the whistle fall from her mouth to dangle on its chain, her face white, her hair floating like a dark shroud around her. She was letting her head flop forward the way Frank's had. But he had her and was pulling her. Telling her to kick, to stay afloat, not to give in. "*Try*," he begged. "*Try*."

"So cold," she said. "I'm so cold."

Then he saw the second wave, not as big as the one that had swept along the *Titanic*'s deck; smaller, lifted probably by the ship's sinking. There were things in it, things rushing at them. He saw the heavy piece of wood and he swiveled Pegeen so he was between her and it, and it smashed him on the head, blinding him with pain. He still had Pegeen, though.

"Lifeboat!" she yelled, and through the dizziness and pain he saw something high on the wave that looked like a raft with people clinging to it, people on top of it. A collapsible lifeboat, but upside down. It was going to sweep right by them.

"Help us!" he shouted to the person kneeling on top of it, the raft rider, and

< 232 >

he thrust Pegeen forward and saw her hauled up; reached for the boat's edge and felt himself heaved up, too. Felt nothing else.

They were on the keel of the upside-down lifeboat, twenty or thirty people crouching or kneeling on its curved, wide bottom. The overturned boat was so heavy with them that water slopped over the sides, ran off the gentle slope. Barry was leaning against someone . . . Pegeen. He moved and she put a hand on his shoulder.

"Barry, you've come to. Thank God. But don't shift like that, you'll have us all in the ocean." She bent over him and wiped his face with the sleeve of her wet coat. "You're bleeding all over your poor face. The stitches have come apart. And there's another big gash under your hair." She touched it with fingers that tried to be careful, but that hurt so much he jerked away.

What were those sounds all around them? Like a flock of starlings in the field at home, scolding as they took off into the sky.

Barry turned his head. All those

< 233 >

people, floating still, their voices so weak and faint. No other boat but their own in the strange, white star-filled sea, flat and calm except for two small gleaming mountains in the distance. For a second he thought they were Slieve Moran and Slieve Tor and he was home looking out of his bedroom window across Pinter's meadow at the gentle hills beyond. But he was somewhere on an ocean, and those were icebergs like the one that had sunk the *Titanic*. All those people—starlings, crying for help. Again he tried to move. "Can't we save them?" he asked.

"We have no paddles," Pegeen whispered. "We're drifting away. Oh, my darling brothers, my poor Jonnie . . . my poor Frank . . . my friend Mary." She was crying quietly, her tears dropping onto Barry's cheek.

He remembered Frank suddenly, his open eyes staring down into the sea. At least she hadn't seen him. At least that much.

"There's no room on this boat anyway," a man beside them said, a big man in a wet, slimy fur coat that he wore over his life jacket. *A bear,* Barry thought.

< 234 >

As if to test them, a hand reached up and grasped the edge of the keel. "Please," a man's voice croaked. The weight of the hand made that side of the boat dip sickeningly, and the bear smacked the clutching fingers with a metal canteen he held. "Go away," he growled. "Do you want to drown us all?"

Pegeen leaned forward, pulling on the edge of the bear's coat. "Let him on, please."

"He's gone," the bear said. "We're all goners, if you want to know the truth. It's just a matter of time."

"Good luck, then, lads," a faint voice from the water said.

"You beast," Pegeen cried weakly, thumping her hand on the bear's boots.

"Where are the other lifeboats?" Barry whispered to her. "Can't they . . . ?"

"They're away," she said. "Far away by now. They never came back."

"Is this all of us that were saved?" Barry asked.

"All," Pegeen said.

Barry lay looking up at the sky. It seemed to close in on him, then drift away as far as heaven itself. Sometimes the sky

< 235 >

and all the stars in it spun in circles. He turned his head. Not so many cries now. The birds had flown away. He frowned. But weren't a lot of them still sleeping, dark on the water? Big white birds, bigger than seagulls, frozen birds. Was one of them a Mick Kelly bird, snug in his white life jacket? Things drifted by them. A striped red-and-white barber pole, a wicker chair. The night was white and the sea, too, filled with jiggling slabs of ice.

There was coughing on their little up-turned boat. There was retching, the splash of vomit spilling overboard into the sea. His head throbbed. It felt as though the top of it were missing.

The sea was getting choppier. It splashed spray on them. Their little boat seemed to wallow. Sometimes his mind cleared, and when it did he didn't like it. He'd lost his gloves somewhere . . . Grandpop's gloves. One of them he remembered letting go when he took out the knife. Lost the gloves. Lost Grandpop.

He thought of the *Titanic* lying at the bottom of the ocean. Bubbles would be coming out of her, drifting lazily up, the

< 236 >

way they came from his toy boat the time
he sank it in the fishpond. He imagined
the colonel still upright on the deck. But
that couldn't be . . . Mr. and Mrs. Goldstein and Arthur asleep on their deck
chairs, the fish swimming furiously around
them. Mrs. Cherry Hat, nice Malcolm,
Scollins. Did he make it through the wave?

"Is Scollins on here with us?" he asked
Pegeen. "Or Watley?" But Pegeen
couldn't seem to hear him, even though
he asked twice and she had her ear next to
his mouth. He felt her shivering against
him. He heard the rasp of her breathing.
She kept stroking his hair, drying off the
water that splashed on him, wiping away
her own tears.

Watley had known he wouldn't be
saved, Barry thought. Was he still holding
the green-and-gold box, or was it drifting
on the ocean, the caul inside still; and
when the wood soaked through, would
the caul spread itself like an invisible net
on the water?

Pegeen talked to him a lot and sometimes he understood her, but sometimes
her words drifted away before his mind

< 237 >

could take hold of them. Mostly she talked about her family, the time Jonnie stole the hat from McKee's window, that time when they caught him. Their mother had had a baby, newborn, then. Something about the baptism and her ma with no hat. Something about McKee, the draper. Barry saw McKee's in his mind, saw the main street in Mullinmore. A fair day and the cattle all brought in for market. She was saying something about the magistrate. "The magistrate told Jonnie, 'One more time and it's jail for you, my boy, or out of the country entirely.' And then that old fellow that drives the carriage for your grandfather, Jonnie just looking at the carriage, he loved the shine and the grandness of it. Your grandfather's man, lifting his whip, and Jonnie putting the big scratch on the side of the shining carriage. It was wrong." Pegeen sobbing big gulps of sobs and Barry trying to touch her, but she seemed so far away. "Sorry," he said. But she was too far away. He saw the silver gleam of the brooch at her neck, the one that held her mother's hair.

"And now Jonnie's dead, drowned.

< 238 >

Jonnie and Frank both, and all the others. My poor ma."

He thought he heard a splash at the back of the upturned boat. Somebody said, "It's the stoker. Poor lad, he jumped off the stern." Somebody else said, "It's well for him to go. His burns are that bad."

Pegeen was keening like a dog locked out in the cold.

Poor stoker, Barry thought. *Poor Jonnie, poor Frank, poor all of them, the ones kept below who never had a chance.*

"No chance in their living, no chance in their dying," he said to Pegeen. "It will be different in America." But she didn't seem to understand that either. *I can make it different,* he thought, *because I know the way it is and the way it can't be anymore.*

Somebody gave him a sip of something from a flask. It was the bear man. There was essence of peppermint in the silver bottle. Grandmother gave him essence of peppermint when he had a cold.

Somebody else was trying to get onto their boat. Was somebody else still alive?

"Help," a voice said.

< 239 >

"We've lost two. There's room for another one."

"Who . . . ?" Barry asked Pegeen, but all she said was, "Rest, Barry. Rest, love." He knew she said "love," he'd heard it. He didn't think he was wrong about that.

The boat rocked dangerously as the person clambered on. Pegeen held Barry tight.

"It's Bride. Bride from the Marconi Room," someone said.

"I've been hanging underneath," Bride said. "All this time. There's air in there to breathe. I was clinging to the seats." He was shaking.

The bear gave him a drink of peppermint essence. A man gave him his own knitted cap and said, "You're half-frozen, son. I can do without this."

Barry wished he had the cap. He was so cold, so deathly cold. He remembered Bride from the Marconi Room. Someone said, "He was the one who sent those SOS messages." *Save Our Ship*, Barry thought. But no one had saved it.

"The *Carpathia*'s on her way." Bride's teeth rattled; his voice came in

< 240 >

frozen spurts. "She got our message before we sank. She'll be here by daybreak. If we can stay afloat . . ."

"We'll have to work at it," a voice in front said. And someone asked, "Work how, Mr. Lightoller?"

"Officer Lightoller's at the bow. He's taken charge," Pegeen whispered. "The water's coming over the keel. There has to be a way to keep the boat balanced or we'll overturn."

"Everybody stand up," Lightoller said. "Careful, careful."

"My friend can't stand," Pegeen shouted.

"I know that. You stay with him. Anybody who can, get on your feet slowly. Don't sink us. We have to keep this boat level or she'll turn over. If it dips one way, we lean the other. It's live or die."

The upturned boat rocked, and then Barry heard Lightoller shouting, "Lean to the left . . . Stand upright . . . Lean to the right . . ." He said it over and over. Barry's eyes were so salt crusted he could only open them halfway. When he did he could make no sense of what he saw. It was as if

< 241 >

the people were doing some crazy dance, standing in a double row on the keel of the boat, swaying this way and that all night long while the stars above them danced, too. There was no other sound in the world but Lightoller's voice and the sloshing of the sea, and it all around them, and over them, over their legs, over their feet.

The stars were disappearing and the sky was changing in color from gray to pink. Barry kept feeling for his legs. Would he ever be able to walk on them again?

Green stars now splashing the sky, one after the other. Exploding. How could stars be green? Pretty, though. He tried to point.

"She's coming, lads."

"It's the *Carpathia*." There was an exhausted cheer.

"She's picked up the other boats. We'll be next."

Pegeen leaned across him. "Barry. Barry O'Neill, we're to be saved, you and I. Hold on now. Don't die on me, for you're all I'll have of Ireland in this new, strange land."

< 242 >

Barry licked his cracked lips, opened his bristly eyes. A large steamer, smoke billowing from her funnels, was coming toward them.

"Glory! Glory be!" Pegeen whispered, and her tears dropped on his upturned face.

He saw her in the sky's morning glow, a light about her as if someone had drawn her outline with a bright, shining pencil.

"I'm to be living in the Bronx," she said. "All the night long you've been talking about Brooklyn and your mother and father waiting."

He didn't remember.

The whistle he'd bought and hung around her neck so long, long ago gleamed silver. He lifted a finger and touched it.

"I don't know where either place is," he whispered. "But blow this. Wherever I am, I'll come."

She smiled.

This time he knew she'd heard.

< 243 >

The Cunard liner *Carpathia* picked up all the survivors from the lifeboats. There were 705 saved. It was 8:30 A.M. The *Carpathia* was close to where the *Titanic* had gone down. Captain Arthur Henry Rostron later reported that he saw "a lot of small broken-up stuff—nothing in the way of anything large." He saw "one body floating with a preserver on." That was all. Estimates of those lost when the RMS *Titanic* sank are uncertain and vary from 1,490 to 1,517.

The day after the sinking, the steamer *Prinz Adelbert* of the Hamburg American

< 245 >

Line passed a large iceberg. On one side, red paint "which had the appearance of having been made by the scraping of a vessel on the iceberg" was plainly visible. They watched as, scarred but otherwise unharmed, the iceberg sailed on.

< 246 >